THE
KINGFISHER TREASURY OF
Bedtime Stories

CHOSEN BY NORA CLARKE
ILLUSTRATED BY ANNABEL SPENCELEY

KING*f*ISHER

NEW YORK

CONTENTS

KINGFISHER TREASURIES

A wealth of stories to share!

Ideal for reading aloud with younger children, or for more experienced readers to enjoy independently, **Kingfisher Treasuries** offer a wonderful range of the very best writing for children. Carefully selected by an expert compiler, each collection reflects the real interests and enthusiasms of children. Stories by favorite classic and contemporary authors appear alongside traditional folk tales and fables in a lively mix of writing drawn from many cultures around the world.

Generously illustrated throughout, **Kingfisher Treasuries** guarantee hours of the highest quality entertainment and, by introducing them to new authors, encourage children to further develop their reading tastes.

KINGFISHER
Larousse Kingfisher Chambers Inc.
80 Maiden Lane
New York, New York 10038
www.lkcpub.com

First published in 1993
6 8 10 9 7 5
5TR / 0501 / THOM / (MA) / 115INDWF

LIBRARY OF CONGRESS CATALOGING–IN–PUBLICATION DATA
The Kingfisher treasury of bedtime stories/illustrated by Annabel Spenceley:
chosen by Nora Clarke. – 1st American ed.
p. cm.
Summary: A collection of twenty stories, most of which are
traditional tales from various countries.
1. Tales. [1. Folklore.] I. Clarke, Nora. M. II. Spenceley, Annabel, ill.
PZ8.1.T695 1993 398.2–dc20 [E] 92-43152 CIP AC

ISBN 1-85697-931-8
Printed in India

Acknowledgments

For permission to reproduce copyright material acknowledgment and thanks are due to the following:

Penguin Books Ltd. for "Olga da Polga and the Night of the Long Dance," from *Olga da Polga Meets Her Match* by Michael Bond, copyright © Michael Bond, 1973. Published by Puffin Books. Pixel Publishing (Australia) for "Jane's Mansion" by Robin Klein, from *Story Chest*, published by Viking Kestrel (1986). Methuen Children's Books for "Number Twelve" by Leila Berg, from *Tales for Telling*. Hutchinson for "Mr. Pepperpot Buys Macaroni" by Alf Prøyson, from *Mrs. Pepperpot Stories*. The Anita Hewett Estate for "Red Umbrella and Yellow Scarf" by Anita Hewett, from *The Anita Hewett Animal Story Book*, published by The Bodley Head (1972). Scholastic Publications Ltd. for "How the Tortoise was Defeated by His Own Magic" by Peggy Appiah, from *Tales of an Ashanti Father*, copyright © Peggy Appiah 1969. Alfred A. Knopf, Inc. for "The Pudding Like a Night on the Sea" by Ann Cameron, from *The Stories Julian Tells*, text copyright © Ann Cameron 1981.

"Black Hook and The Skunk" and "Tattercoats" copyright © Nora Clarke 1993.
"Mollie Whuppie" copyright © Susan Price 1993.

Stories retold from traditional sources that in this collection are © Grisewood & Dempsey Ltd. are as follows:
"Snow White and the Seven Dwarfs," "Sleeping Beauty" and "Rumpelstiltskin" retold by Linda Yeatman.
"Thunder and Lightning's New Home," "The Emperor's New Clothes," and "The Golden Goose" retold by Nora Clarke. "Po-wan and Kuan-yin" retold by Eugenie Summerfield. "The Husband Who Looked After the House" retold by Deborah Manley.

Every effort has been made to obtain permission from copyright holders. If, regrettably, any omissions have been made, we shall be pleased to make suitable corrections in any reprint.

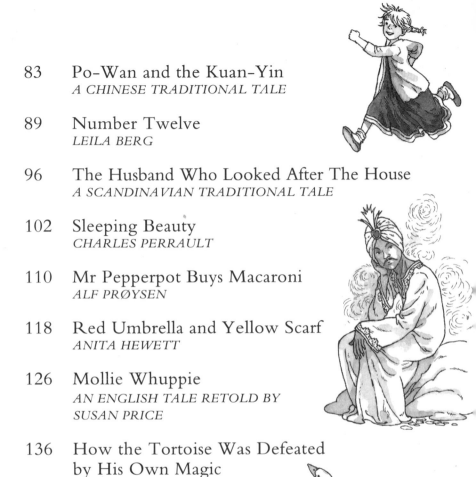

SNOW WHITE
AND THE
SEVEN DWARFS

Grimm Brothers

One winter's day, when the snow was falling, a beautiful queen sat sewing by a window. As she looked out onto the white garden, she saw a black raven, and while she watched it, she accidentally pricked her finger with the needle. When she saw the drop of blood, she thought to herself, "How wonderful it would be if I could have a little girl with skin as white as snow, hair as black as a raven, and lips as red as this drop of blood."

Not long afterward the queen did have a baby daughter, and when she saw her jet black hair, her snow-white skin, and her red, red lips, she remembered her wish and called her Snow White.

Snow White grew up to be a pretty child, but sadly, after a few years, her mother died and her father married again. Snow White's stepmother was a beautiful woman, too, but she was very vain.

More than anything else, she wanted to be certain that she was the most beautiful woman in the world. She had a magic mirror, and every day she would look at her reflection and say:

"Mirror, mirror, on the wall,
Who is the fairest one of all?"

The mirror would always reply:

"You, O, Queen, are the fairest one of all."

The queen would smile when she heard this, for she knew the mirror never failed to speak the truth.

The years passed. Each year Snow White grew prettier and prettier, until one day, when her stepmother looked in the magic mirror and asked:

"Mirror, mirror, on the wall,
Who is the fairest one of all?"

the mirror replied:

"You, O, Queen, are fair, 'tis true,
But Snow White is fairer now than you."

The queen was angry and jealous. In a terrible rage she decided that Snow White must be killed.

She called for a hunter and told him to take Snow White deep into the forest and to kill her. To prove that Snow White was indeed dead, she then commanded him to cut out Snow White's heart and bring it back to her. The hunter was very sad. Like everyone in the king's household, he loved Snow White, but he knew he must obey the queen's orders. So the next day, he took Snow White into the forest, but, as he drew his knife, Snow White fell to her knees.

"Please spare my life," she begged. "Leave me here. I'll never return to the palace, I promise." The hunter agreed gladly. He was sure the queen would never know he had disobeyed her. He killed a young deer, cut out its heart, and took it to the queen, pretending it was Snow White's heart.

Poor Snow White wandered through the forest feeling tired, lonely, and hungry. At last, she came to a little house standing in the middle of a clearing. Hoping that she might be able to find shelter, she walked up and knocked at the door. When there was no reply, she opened it and went in.

Inside she saw a room, all spick-and-span, with a long table laid with seven places – seven knives and forks, seven wooden plates, and seven drinking cups. On the plates and in the cups were food and drink. Snow White was so hungry that she took a little food from each plate and a sip from each cup. She did not want to empty one person's plate and cup only.

Beyond the table were seven little beds, all neatly made. She tried out some of them, and when she found one that was comfortable, she fell into a deep sleep.

Now, the cottage was the home of seven dwarfs. All day long they worked in a nearby mine, digging diamonds from deep inside the mountain. When they returned home that evening, they were amazed to see that someone had come into their cottage and had taken some food and drink from each of the places at their table. They were even

more surprised when one of the dwarfs called out that he had found a lovely girl asleep on his bed. The seven dwarfs gathered around her, holding their candles high as they marveled at her beauty. But they decided to leave her sleeping, for they were kind men.

The next morning, Snow White told the dwarfs her story. When they realized that Snow White had nowhere to go, they asked her whether she would like to stay with them in their cottage in the forest.

"With all my heart," replied Snow White, happy that she now had a home.

The dwarfs were worried that Snow White's stepmother might find out that Snow White was still alive. They warned Snow White to be wary of strangers whenever she was alone in the cottage.

Back at the palace, the queen was delighted to hear that Snow White had been killed. Confident that she was once more the most beautiful woman in the world, she looked in her magic mirror and said:

"Mirror, mirror, on the wall,
Who is the fairest one of all?"

To her horror, the mirror replied:

"You, O, Queen, are fair, 'tis true,
But Snow White is fairer still than you."

The queen trembled with anger as she realized that the hunter had tricked her. She decided that she would now find Snow White and kill her herself.

Disguised as an old peddler woman with a tray of ribbons and pretty things to sell, the queen went

out into the forest. When she came to the dwarfs'
cottage in the clearing, she knocked. A wicked
smile spread across her face when Snow White
opened the door.

"Why, pretty maid," she said pleasantly, "won't
you buy some of the wares I have to sell? Would
you like some ribbons or buttons, some buckles, or
a new lacing for your dress, perhaps?"

Snow White looked eagerly at the tray.

The queen could see that she was tempted by
the pretty lacing, and so she offered to help tie it on
for her. But she pulled the lacing so tight that Snow
White could not breathe and fell to the floor as if
she were dead. The queen hurried back to her
palace, sure that now she was truly the most
beautiful woman in the world.

When the dwarfs came home that evening, they
found Snow White lying on the floor, deathly pale
and still. Horrified, they gathered round her.

Then one of them
spotted that she had a
new lacing on her
dress and that it was
tied extremely tightly.
Quickly, they cut it,
and immediately Snow
White began to breathe
again and the color
came back to her
cheeks. All the dwarfs

heaved a sigh of relief, as already they had come to love Snow White dearly. They begged her to allow no strangers into the cottage while she was alone. Snow White promised she would do as they said.

Once again, in the palace, the queen asked the mirror:

"*Mirror, mirror, on the wall,*
Who is the fairest one of all?"

And the mirror replied:

"*You, O, Queen, are fair, 'tis true,*
But Snow White is fairer still than you."

The queen was speechless with rage when she realized that her plan to kill Snow White had failed once more. She made up her mind to try again, and this time she was determined to succeed.

Taking an apple with one rosy-red side and one yellow side, she carefully inserted poison into the red part of the apple. Then, dressed as a peasant woman, she put the apple in a basket and set out into the forest once again.

When she knocked at the cottage door, the queen was quick to explain she had not come to sell anything. She guessed that Snow White would have been warned not to buy anything from a stranger. She simply chatted with Snow White, and, when Snow White more at ease, she offered her an apple as a present. Snow White was tempted, because the rosy apple looked delicious. But she refused, saying she had been told not to accept anything from strangers.

"Let me show you how harmless it is," said the queen. "I will take a bite, and if I come to no harm, you will see it is safe."

But the queen took a bite from the yellow side of the apple, which was not poisoned. Thinking it harmless, Snow White stretched out her hand for the apple and also took a bite, but from the rosy-red side.

No sooner had the apple touched her lips than Snow White fell down as though dead, and that evening, when the dwarfs returned, they were quite unable to revive her. They turned her over to see if her dress had been laced too tightly, but they could find nothing different about her. They watched over her all through the night, but when morning came and she still lay without any sign of life, they decided she must be dead. Weeping bitterly, they laid her in a coffin and placed a glass lid over the top so that all could still admire her beauty. Then they carried the coffin to the top of a hill where they took turns to stand guard over their beautiful Snow White.

The queen was delighted that day when she looked in her mirror and asked:

"Mirror, mirror, on the wall,
Who is the fairest one of all?"

and the mirror replied:

"You, O, Queen, are the fairest one of all."

How cruelly she laughed when she heard those words.

Not long after this, a prince came riding through the forest and came to the hill where Snow White lay in her glass-topped coffin. She looked so beautiful that he fell in love with her at once, and he asked the dwarfs if he might have the coffin and take it to his castle. The dwarfs would

not allow him to do this, for they too loved Snow White. But they did agree to let the prince kiss her.

As the prince gently raised Snow White's head to kiss her, the piece of poisoned apple fell from her lips. She stirred, and then she stretched a little. Slowly, she came back to life. When Snow White saw the handsome prince kneeling on the ground beside her, she, too, fell in love. The seven dwarfs were overjoyed to see her alive once more and in love with a prince, and they wished the two of them a long and happy life together.

Meanwhile, far away in the palace, the queen stood looking at her reflection in the mirror. But then she heard the mirror say:

"You, O Queen, are fair, 'tis true,
But Snow White is fairer still than you."

She was so angry that Snow White had escaped death once more that she took her magic mirror and fled from the palace, never to be seen again.

As for Snow White, she said farewell to her kind friends the dwarfs and rode away on the back of the prince's horse. At his castle they were married, and they both lived happily ever after.

THUNDER AND LIGHTNING'S NEW HOME

A Caribbean folk tale

At one time, many hundreds of years ago, Lightning and Thunder lived upon the Earth. Lightning was a boy with a wicked temper. He struck anybody he didn't like and sometimes set fire to their houses. His mother, Thunder, shouted at him, but her loud voice deafened everybody and made the trees shake.

At last, people began to grumble to the king.

"We are tired of Lightning's temper and Thunder's shouts," they said.

"You'd better live outside the village," the king said to Thunder and Lightning. "Then you cannot upset anyone."

Everything was quiet for a time. Then Lightning started burning houses and trees again, and Thunder scolded him with her loudest, thundery voice.

"They are still bothering us," the people complained to the king.

The king grew angry.

"Thunder and Lightning," he said, "stop annoying everybody. Take yourselves off to the mountains, and do not show yourselves here again."

Thunder and Lightning were furious. Their eyes flashed, but to everyone's surprise, they obeyed and moved off, rumbling and grumbling.

It was peaceful then in the village, but Lightning wanted revenge. One day, he crept back down the mountainside. When he reached the village, he crackled and hissed and set the farmers' corn alight. He kicked tall trees until they split in two. He set fire to the haystacks and farmhouses, and even killed cows and horses in the fields.

Thunder came after her wicked son. She shouted and bellowed, and frightened the people. She shouted so loudly that the ground shook, but Lightning took no notice. He went on flashing and crackling for hours and hours. Thunder screamed and roared until at last both of them were tired out.

The people could take it no longer and rushed off to tell the king.

"You must send Thunder and Lightning far away," they said. "We do not want them anywhere near us."

The king thought long and hard. Then he ordered Thunder and Lightning to come and stand before him.

"Lightning," he said sternly, "you have been very wicked. As for you, Thunder, your big voice frightens us all. From now on, you must both live in the sky."

Thunder and Lightning begged him to relent.

"I promise I'll never be bad-tempered again," hissed Lightning.

"And I'll speak softly," Thunder said. But of course, she could only shout!

"You'll never be able to keep those promises,"

20

the people said. "You've burned our fields and our houses. We cannot forgive you."

"How can you put us up into the sky?" hissed Lightning rudely.

"Wait and see," said the king.

They did not have to wait long. Hundreds of birds flocked around – parakeets from the forest, long-legged flamingos, pelicans, and vultures. They cackled and squawked. Then they picked mother and son up with their claws and beaks and held them tightly. Up, up, up, the birds flew, high above the clouds, and there they left Thunder and Lightning.

The king and the people were sure they would never be troubled again. But Lightning still loses his temper sometimes and sends bright, fiery flashes down to Earth. And a little later, Thunder roars at him. Have you ever heard her?

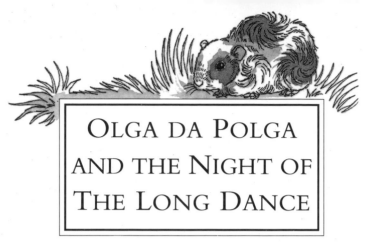

OLGA DA POLGA AND THE NIGHT OF THE LONG DANCE

Michael Bond

*Olga da Polga is a guinea pig with a vivid imagination
and a talent for telling stories. She lives with the
Sawdust family along with Noel the cat, Graham the
tortoise, and Fangio the porcupine.*

"I suppose," said Noel condescendingly, "one
advantage of having short legs is that when the
weather's bad, you can crawl under the nearest
stone and keep dry."

"I'd sooner do that," replied Fangio, "than get
sopping wet every time it rains."

"Who wants long legs anyway?" said Graham
darkly. "I don't. You sometimes see things you'd
rather not. I stood on a molehill once, and I didn't
like what I saw at all. No wonder moles live
underground."

Olga chuckled to herself as she listened to the
conversation on one side of her hutch.

The subject of legs had come up earlier that day
when Fangio happened to make a remark about the

way Noel walked. Noel was a particularly beautiful cat. He was much given to posing – draping himself on tree stumps or the tops of walls in order to show off to the best advantage – but he was proudest of all about the way he walked, and Fangio's comment had set him off.

Although Noel secretly liked to be noticed, he was a little upset by the fact that he had been, and he spent some time listing the countless advantages enjoyed by those who were lucky enough to have long legs, and the many, many drawbacks suffered by those who only had short ones.

Olga chuckled again as she basked in the afternoon sun.

Noel's voice suddenly broke into her day-dreams. "And what's *your* excuse?" he said.

Olga gave a start and looked around the backyard. She hadn't realized they had been joined by someone else, and she wondered who it could possibly be.

"Well?" Noel put his face against the wire.

Olga stared at him. "Are you addressing me?" she asked coldly.

"Your legs are so short," said Noel, "I can't even see them."
Slowly and carefully, Olga drew herself up to her full height until she was almost standing on tiptoe. "I keep them tucked under me for safety," she said. "Besides, I happen to have unusually long fur."

"I suppose being so short has its uses," said Noel, turning back to the others. "I mean, it keeps the place neat. You can sweep up as you go along."

Fangio made a noise which sounded suspiciously like a giggle, but it was quickly suppressed when he saw the look in Olga's eye.

"I admit," Olga sank to the ground because, try as she might, she couldn't hold her pose a moment longer, "I admit that my legs could perhaps do with being a trifle longer – *if* I wanted to go around on stilts. But at least we guinea pigs know what it's like to have long legs. We haven't always been like this.

We guinea pigs used to have the most beautiful legs imaginable. Long and slender and . . ."

"When was that?" demanded Noel. "I've never seen a guinea pig with long legs."

"Oh, it was a long time ago," said Olga vaguely. "It was in Russia."

"Russia?" repeated Noel. "Guinea pigs don't come from Russia."

"We may not *come* from there," said Olga, "but we've *been* there. You'll find guinea pigs wherever they value breeding and good looks and . . ."

"Oh, *do* get on with it," exclaimed Noel impatiently. In truth, he was feeling a little put out that his afternoon's entertainment at the expense of Fangio and Graham had been interrupted.

Olga took a deep breath. "For this story," she said, "you will have to try and picture yourself living in Russia at the time of the Revolution.

"In those days, the Tzar kept hundreds of guinea pigs for his special pleasure, and they were said to have the longest and most beautiful legs of any animal in the world.

"For a long time," she added as an afterthought, "they did try to breed some cats with legs half as long, but they never quite succeeded. Something always seemed to go wrong. They either bent the wrong way at the knees or else they fell off . . ."

Noel gave a loud snort.

"After the Revolution," continued Olga hurriedly, "the people who had taken over the palace didn't know quite what to do to pass the time. They weren't used to the life, you see, and they soon got fed up with listening to ballylaikas all day . . ."

"Don't you mean *bala*laikas?" asked Noel suspiciously. Rooting around in trash cans as he did, Noel was apt to know about these things.

"If you'd had to listen to them all day long, you'd have called them *bally*laikas, too," said Olga.

"Anyway, at last, when they could stand it no longer, their leader called on the Royal Guinea Pigs to entertain them.

"At first the guinea pigs didn't know what to do. Usually, it was *they* who were entertained and not the other way around. But like guinea pigs the world over, they were very gifted. The problem really was to decide which of their many talents would be most suitable.

"And then the sound of the music gave them an idea. Having such long and beautiful legs, they were particularly good dancers, so that's what they did. They danced. Not the kind of dancing

26

we know today, but special Russian dancing. They stood on their hind legs, and they folded their front paws across their chests, and away they went.

"The audience had never seen anything like it.

" 'Moreski!' they cried. 'Moreski! Moreski!'

"And the louder they called out, the faster the musicians played; and the faster the musicians played, the faster the guinea pigs had to dance. On and on it went. On into the night – hour after hour."

"Show us some," broke in Fangio.

Olga gave him a long, hard look. Really, she wondered for a moment whose side he was on – hers or Noel's. "I will," she said at last, "after that airplane has passed over. It really is most distracting."

"What airplane?" asked Noel.

"The one behind you," said Olga.

Olga's audience turned and looked up at the sky.

"I can't see any airplane," said Noel, as they turned back again.

"It was going very fast," said Olga. "It was going almost as fast as the dance I just did for you."

The others stared back at her in disbelief.

"Well, now the airplane *has* gone," said Noel, "perhaps you can do it for us again."

"It's a bit difficult on grass," replied Olga, playing for time.

"There's a bare patch right behind you," said Graham.

Olga suddenly gave a quick shuffle. "Tarrraaaaaaa!" she exclaimed, as a small cloud of dust rose into the air.

"Was that it?" demanded Noel scornfully.

"I didn't see a thing," said Fangio.

"Nor me," agreed Graham.

Olga gave a deep, deep sigh. "Russian dancing is very quick," she said. "If you *will* look the other way or blink every time, I'm afraid you'll never see it.

"Now," she said wearily, "I *must* get on with my story. Really, all this dancing has quite worn me out.

"Dawn," she continued, "was beginning to break when gradually the audience in the Tzar's palace noticed a very strange thing. In the beginning they'd been able to look out from their seats straight at the dancers; now they were looking down on them.

"The guinea pigs," said Olga dramatically, "had danced so much they'd worn out their legs – right down to the ground.

"And that's why, to this very day, guinea pigs, although they have very beautiful legs, also have rather short ones."

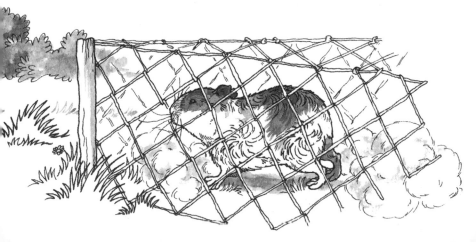

The others fell silent for a moment or two, and Olga took the opportunity to go back to enjoying the sunshine, closing her eyes and snuggling down into the warm grass.

"Look," Noel banged on the side of her hutch with his tail, "if they stood on their back legs like you said, and danced them away, why haven't guinea pigs got great big front ones still?"

"Hear! Hear!" echoed Fangio and Graham.

Olga opened one eye and put on her pained expression. There were some questions she just didn't choose to answer.

"If you don't mind," she said, "I happen to be fast asleep."

THE EMPEROR'S NEW CLOTHES

Hans Christian Andersen

There was once an emperor who was very vain. He loved to wear expensive clothes, and he tried to look as splendid as possible all the time. In his palace he had many rooms full of closets and chests, all packed with fine clothes. He would spend hours admiring himself in long mirrors every time he changed, which he did several times a day. Cloth merchants and tailors grew rich by supplying clothes to the emperor, and many beautifully colored and finely woven materials were imported from far and near for the emperor to choose from. Many people laughed at him for his vanity, but he was too proud to notice.

One day, two swindlers, pretending to be cloth merchants, came to the palace and asked to see the emperor. They told the servants they had come from a faraway land with cloth more beautiful than anything the emperor had ever seen before. When the palace servants asked to see the cloth, they were told it was for the emperor's eyes alone.

The emperor was so excited when he heard about the visitors that he arranged to see them immediately. Bowing low before him, the two swindlers said that they had come to offer him the finest material in the whole world. It was so fine, they told him, that it had the magical quality of being invisible to anyone who was a fool. The emperor asked to see it at once, so the two scoundrels opened their big wooden trunk and pretended to take out first one roll of cloth and then another. The emperor blinked, for he could see no cloth at all, even though the men did look as if they were unrolling something.

"I cannot let them think I am a fool," he thought to himself, so he pretended he could see the material perfectly well.

"Look at these most beautiful colors!" said one scoundrel.

"And the fine gold thread!" said the other, as they held up the invisible cloth before the emperor.

"Yes," said the emperor, sounding as enthusiastic as he could. "The colors are beautiful and the design magnificent."

He called in his wife and the chief minister along with some of the courtiers to admire the cloth, and he explained about its magic qualities. They, too, could see no cloth at all, but they did not want the emperor to think they were fools, so one by one they all admired the cloth. The emperor was slightly disappointed because he had always thought that his wife and the chief minister were rather foolish. But when they admired the material and talked about it, even putting out their hands to touch it, he decided he must have been wrong about them all the time. And if they could see the material, he certainly wasn't going to announce that he could not.

"Would Your Majesty like us to take your measurements so that a suit can be made for you from these fine materials?" the merchants asked. "We will make it ourselves, for we cannot trust anybody else to cut and stitch it."

The emperor agreed to have a suit made and promised to reward the merchants well with money and jewels.

The scoundrels were given a room in the palace for their work. One material was chosen for the jacket, another for the trousers. A special shirt with a lace collar and cuffs was also to be made from the material in the merchants' chest. The emperor was very particular about where he wanted the buttons and how tight the waist was to be, and the scoundrels fussed around him, making careful notes of all his wishes.

A few days later, the emperor went to try on his new suit. He took off all his clothes and allowed the merchants to dress him, although he could not see what they were putting on. Then he walked across to the long mirror. He turned round and round, but he could see no clothes at all. He called his chief minister, who was astonished to see the emperor standing before him with no clothes on, but not wishing to appear a fool, he said, "How magnificent Your Majesty looks. How splendid! Why not wear this wonderful suit of new clothes at your birthday procession next week?"

"The chief minister is not such a fool after all!" thought the emperor, and agreed that he would wear the clothes when he rode through the city at the head of the great procession.

Around the city, the news spread that the emperor would be wearing the finest clothes ever seen for his birthday procession, and when the time came, the crowds gathered in the streets to see him. They had also heard that only wise people could see the new clothes, which, to fools, would be invisible, and everyone had secretly decided that they would rather pretend to see them than let their friends and neighbors think they were fools.

The emperor dressed with great care on the day, flicking specks of dust off the wonderful new clothes he could not see, and admiring himself in the mirror for even longer than usual until the master of ceremonies came to say that the crowds were growing impatient. It was time for the procession to begin.

As he rode through the streets, the emperor heard the crowds cheering, and thought, "How lucky I am to rule over so many wise people. It seems there are no fools in my country, for everyone can see my new clothes."

But there was one small boy who had climbed a tree to get a better view of the emperor. He had not heard that the emperor's clothes were only visible to wise people, and he shouted out at once, "What has happened to all his clothes? The emperor isn't wearing anything at all!"

The crowd laughed uneasily. Then someone else shouted out,

"The boy's right! The emperor has no clothes on!"

The people's laughter turned on the emperor and then on themselves, for they realized that they had all been fools to believe the story of the magic clothes.

The emperor was very angry with the scoundrels who had tricked him and sent for them as soon as he got back to the palace. But they had already fled, taking with them all the money and jewels the emperor had given them. And you may be sure they were never seen in that country again.

Then the emperor sent for the little boy who had called out that he could not see the clothes. He told the boy he was the only wise person in the whole country, for he alone was not afraid to speak the truth, and that when he grew up he would make him chief minister.

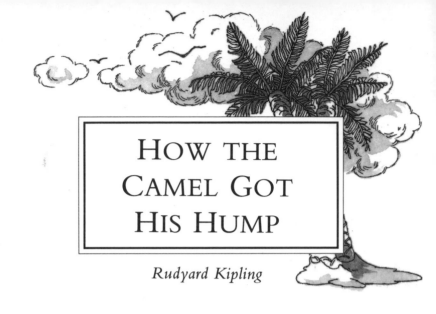

HOW THE CAMEL GOT HIS HUMP

Rudyard Kipling

N ow this is the next tale, and it tells how the Camel got his big hump.

In the beginning of years, when the world was so new-and-all and the Animals were just beginning to work for Man, there was a Camel, and he lived in the middle of a Howling Desert because he did not want to work; and besides, he was a Howler himself. So he ate sticks and thorns and tamarisks and milkweed and prickles, most 'scruciatingly idle; and when anybody spoke to him he said, "Humph!" Just "Humph!" and no more.

Presently the Horse came to him on Monday morning, with a saddle on his back and a bit in his mouth, and said, "Camel, O Camel, come out and trot like the rest of us."

"Humph!" said the Camel, and the Horse went away and told the Man.

Presently the Dog came to him, with a stick in his mouth, and said, "Camel, O Camel, come and fetch and carry like the rest of us."

"Humph!" said the Camel, and the Dog went away and told the Man.

Presently the Ox came to him, with the yoke on his neck, and said, "Camel, O Camel, come and plow like the rest of us."

"Humph!" said the Camel, and the Ox went away and told the Man.

At the end of the day, the Man called the Horse and the Dog and the Ox together and said, "Three, O Three, I'm very sorry for you (with the world so new-and-all); but that Humph-thing in the Desert can't work or he would have been here by now, so I am going to leave him alone, and you must work double-time to make up for it."

That made the Three very angry (with the world so new-and-all), and they held a palaver, and an *indaba*, and a *punchayet*, and a powwow on the edge of the Desert; and the Camel came chewing milkweed *most* 'scruciatingly idle and laughed at them. Then he said, "Humph!" and went away again.

Presently there came along the Djinn in charge of All Deserts, rolling in a cloud of dust (Djinns always travel that way because it is Magic), and he stopped to palaver and powwow with the Three.

"Djinn of All Deserts," said the Horse, "*is* it right for anyone to be idle, with the world so new-and-all?"

"Certainly not," said the Djinn.

"Well," said the Horse, "there's a thing in the middle of your Howling Desert (and he's a Howler himself) with a long neck and long legs, and he hasn't done a stroke of work since Monday morning. He won't trot."

"Whew!" said the Djinn, whistling. "That's my Camel, for all the gold in Arabia! What does he say about it?"

"He says, 'Humph!'" said the Dog; "and he won't fetch and carry."

"Does he say anything else?"

"Only 'Humph!'; and he won't plow," said the Ox.

"Very good," said the Djinn. "I'll humph him if you will kindly wait a minute."

The Djinn rolled himself up in his dust-cloak
and took a bearing across the Desert, and found the
Camel most 'scruciatingly idle, looking at his own
reflection in a pool of water.

"My long and bubbling friend," said the Djinn, "what's this I hear of your doing no work, with the world so new-and-all?"

"Humph!" said the Camel.

The Djinn sat down with his chin in his hand and began to think a Great Magic, while the Camel looked at his own reflection in the pool of water.

"You've given the Three extra work ever since Monday morning, all on account of your 'scruciating idleness," said the Djinn; and he went on thinking Magics, with his chin in his hand.

"Humph!" said the Camel.

"I shouldn't say that again if I were you," said the Djinn; "you might say it once too often. Bubbles, I want you to work."

And the Camel said, "Humph!" again; but no sooner had he said it than he saw his back, that he was so proud of, puffing up and puffing up into a great big lolloping humph.

"Do you see that?" said the Djinn. "That's your very own humph that you've brought upon your very own self by not working. Today is Thursday

42

and you've done no work since Monday, when the work began. Now you are going to work."

"How can I," said the Camel, "with this humph on my back?"

"That's made a-purpose," said the Djinn, "all because you missed those three days. You will be able to work now for three days without eating, because you can live on your humph; and don't you ever say I never did anything for you. Come out of the Desert and go to the Three, and behave. 'Humph', yourself!"

And the Camel humphed himself, humph and all, and went away to join the Three. And from that day to this, the Camel always wears a humph (we call it a "hump" now, not to hurt his feelings); but he has never yet caught up with the three days that he missed at the beginning of the world, and he has never yet learned how to behave.

JANE'S MANSION

Robin Klein

Jane liked pretending to be grander than she really was. One day, she was walking home from school with a new girl named Kylie and showing off as usual.

"We have five Siamese cats at our house. And a special lemonade fountain."

Kylie dawdled, hoping to be invited in.

"I'd ask you in," said Jane, "but my mother's overseas. She's a famous opera singer."

"Wow!" said Kylie.

"She's singing in Paris. Our housekeeper, Mrs. Grid, is looking after me. Our house has twenty-five rooms full of Persian carpets and antique furniture."

Kylie looked at Jane's house, thinking that a house containing such splendors would somehow look different.

"Don't take any notice of the front view," said Jane. "My dad built it like that to trick burglars. Inside it's different. My father is a millionaire."

She waved goodbye airily and went inside.

The house certainly was different inside!

The living-room was carpeted with gorgeous rugs, and had a silver fountain labeled "ice-cold lemonade". The cane furniture had been replaced by carved oak.

"*Mom*! Did we win the lottery?" Jane yelled excitedly! Her mother wasn't home, but a note had been left in the kitchen. It read:

FROM PARIS GOING
TO MILAN TO SING
TOSCA, AFTER
THAT VIENNA.
HOUSEKEEPER WILL
LOOK AFTER YOU,
LOVE, MOM.

Jane read the note and then phoned the factory where her dad worked. A voice said, "Sorry, it's not possible to speak to Mr. Lawson. He's overseas inspecting all his oil wells, diamond mines, and banks."

It was Jane's turn to say "wow!"

She went into her room to change. Normally, her room was a clutter of dropped clothes, unmade bed, and overdue library books. But now it was magnificent. It had a four-poster bed, and a TV set in the ceiling. Jane was so impressed that she hung up her dress in the closet instead of letting it lie like a puddle on the floor.

She ran all around the splendid house, looking at everything. It was amazing that such a vast mansion could fit into an ordinary suburban home. The backyard was too stupendous to be called that. There was a sunken pool in a huge lawn. She couldn't even find the fences that separated her house from the neighbors'. "Not that I'd want to, now that I'm a millionaire's daughter," she thought smugly.

At six, a brass gong summoned her for dinner at a long table lit by a candelabra. There was one place set.

"Don't put your elbows on the table, Miss Jane," somebody strict said. It was Mrs. Grid, the housekeeper, and she was just as impressive as the house.

Jane couldn't even resist showing off to her. "I've got to go to the Youth Club," she said when she had finished dinner. "I won every single trophy. It's Presentation Night."

"I'll have Norton bring the car around to the front door," Mrs. Grid said.

Jane waited by the front steps. A huge car drove up, and a uniformed man held the door open for her. Jane remembered telling Kylie that she had a chauffeur. She felt very important being driven to Youth Club like that. Everyone's parents had come for Presentation Night. She regretted that hers were overseas, specially when the club president announced, "Trophy for the most advanced member – Jane Lawson."

No sooner had Jane received the trophy and sat down than the president said, "Cup awarded for callisthenics – Jane Lawson," and she had to go back. She won every single prize, but it wasn't nearly as nice as she thought it would be. After her tenth trip to the stage, the clapping sounded forced, and most of the parents were glaring at her.

When she got home she showed the trophies to Mrs. Grid.

Mrs. Grid only said, "All that silver will take a lot of polishing. I've already got enough to do looking after this mansion."

The next morning her father cabled that he was in Brazil buying coffee plantations. Jane rang Kylie to brag.

"My dad bought me a pair of skates," Kylie said excitedly. "Want to come over and see?"

"Skates are nothing," Jane scoffed. "*My* father bought *me* a *horse*."

There was a loud neighing at the window, and she hung up the phone and went to look. A large horse was trotting around in the yard.

"Put your horse back in the stable at once," said Mrs. Grid crossly.

"I don't want to," said Jane. But Mrs. Grid looked at her so sternly that she lied quickly, "We have a groom to look after my horse."

A bandy-legged man in jodhpurs appeared and led the horse away. Jane was relieved, because she was really scared of horses.

She went for another walk around her mansion, finding a whole lot of things she'd lied into existence in past conversations

with people. There was a trained circus poodle, a crystal bathtub with goldfish swimming around the sides, a real little theater complete with spotlights, a gymnasium in the basement, and five Siamese cats. She had a marvelous time playing with all that, but she was starting to feel lonely. Mrs. Grid

was too busy and crotchety to be company. Jane rang Kylie again.

"Come over and I'll let you ride my horse," she offered.

"You wouldn't come over to see my skates," Kylie pointed out, offended.

"We've got a real theater and a crystal bathtub with goldfish swimming around the sides. Please come round to my house and play," Jane begged.

"I'd better not," said Kylie.

"Why not?"

"Your house sounds too grand. I'd be scared of breaking something valuable. I'd better just play with you at school." She hung up.

Jane sat and looked at all her trophies and tried to feel proud. But she knew very well she hadn't really won any of those glittering things. She'd only got them by lying.

She missed her parents dreadfully. She remembered that this weekend her dad had intended to make her a treehouse, but he was in Brazil instead.

"Where's my shell collection and my pig I made out of a lemon?" she asked Mrs. Grid, starting to cry.

"I threw all that trash out," said Mrs. Grid. "And there's no point moping. Your parents have to work very hard to keep you in the manner you prefer. You'll just have to wait till Christmas to see them. I daresay they'll be able to drop in for a few minutes then."

"I'm getting my own speedboat for Christmas," Jane boasted, lying automatically through her tears.

"That reminds me," said Mrs. Grid. "This telegram arrived for you."

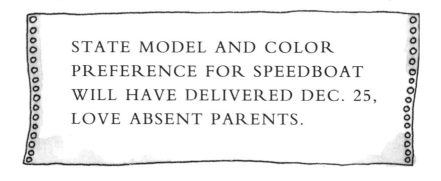

STATE MODEL AND COLOR PREFERENCE FOR SPEEDBOAT WILL HAVE DELIVERED DEC. 25, LOVE ABSENT PARENTS.

Jane bawled louder.

"Just as well you're going away to boarding school tomorrow," Mrs. Grid said. "So I won't have to put up with that awful noise."

Jane was shocked into silence. She remembered lying to the neighbors that she'd won a scholarship to boarding school. She didn't want to go. She wanted her own house to be the way it usually was, with her own nice, comfortable parents in it.

"You could pack your things for boarding

school now," said Mrs. Grid. "I'll get Norton to drive you there early."

Jane jumped up. She ran out of the house and down the street to Kylie's. When Kylie opened the door, Jane babbled feverishly, "We don't have a swimming pool, lemonade fountain, horse, groom, miniature theater, or five Siamese cats, and I'm not going to boarding school. My dad's not a millionaire, he's a fitter and turner. And my mom can't sing for anything. We haven't got any antiques or Persian carpets, and I didn't win any trophies at Youth Club. I'll never tell any more lies ever again! And we haven't got a housekeeper, or a chauffeur called Norton. Please come up to my house to play, Kylie."

"All right," said Kylie. "I knew you were lying, anyhow."

They went back to Jane's house, and Jane drew a big breath and opened the door. It opened into her usual living-room with its old cane furniture, and she could hear her mom in the kitchen, singing off-key. Jane ran and hugged her.

"Where's Dad?" she asked anxiously.

"Just gone up to get the lumber for your treehouse," said her mother. "You can take some scones into your room if you like."

"My room hasn't got a four-poster bed or a TV set in the ceiling," Jane said to Kylie before she opened the door.

"I didn't think it had," said Kylie.

They ate their scones while they looked at
Jane's shell collection and the pig she had made
out of a lemon. The scones tasted much nicer
than Mrs. Grid's cooking.

"We haven't got a gymnasium in the basement
or a poodle or a speedboat either," said Jane. "I tell
a lot of lies."

Her mother came to collect her scone plate.

She was cross about something.

"Who stripped the enamel off the bathtub and
put goldfish in the sides?" she demanded.

BLACK HOOK
AND THE SKUNK

An Algonquin tale

L ong ago there once lived an evil spirit called
Black Hook. Black Hook had the body of a
wolf, he was as strong as the biggest bear, and he
had long black hooks that scared even the bravest of
the native braves. This cruel spirit hated everything
and everybody, but there was one thing that
frightened him. He was terrified of water because
he could not swim. All the animals scampered
helter-skelter when Black Hook was around. . .
Well, nearly all the animals, for there was one
small creature who wasn't afraid of Black Hook.
Who was this, you may ask? None other than
the skunk.

Now it happened one day that this little
creature was sitting on the riverbank smoking his
pipe when Black Hook came rattling along feeling
particularly nasty.

"Grrrhh," cried the evil spirit, when he saw

Skunk, "I'll make you scared of me."

But the skunk calmly went on smoking his pipe and didn't twitch a whisker.

"Rooaaarr! You'd better run before I swing my hooks into you," yelled Black Hook, shaking an ugly claw right under Skunk's little nose.

"Just be on your way, you ugly creature," squeaked Skunk. "I'm enjoying my pipe here by this river, and you are bothering me. Go away."

"What's that?" roared the spirit. "Don't you know who I am? I'll tear you to pieces, you miserable little worm. Then I'll gobble you up and use your skin to polish my hooks. . . Doesn't that scare you?"

"Not very much," replied Skunk.

Black Hook stared. Nobody had ever spoken to him this way before. He picked up an enormous rock. "Let's see how brave you are when I've crunched you up like this," he said, and he broke the rock into a thousand pieces.

"Certainly you seem pretty strong," said Skunk, "but I bet I am stronger." He jumped up and put his pipe down very carefully on the bank.

"Why, I'll flatten you with three hits," boasted Black Hook.

"All right, you go first and then I'll get to work," murmured Skunk.

"If you live long enough!" roared Black Hook as he hit Skunk a terrible blow. Crash! Skunk was knocked into the ground up to his knees. Bang! Skunk sank up to his neck. Wham!

Skunk disappeared completely into a huge hole with the third hit.

"Try hitting me now, you miserable creature," Black Hook roared with laughter.

"Don't worry, I'll get even with you," came a small squeak from the hole, and presently Skunk clambered painfully out, rubbing his little furry head.

"You can't hurt me," shouted Black Hook, who was peeved when he saw he had not killed Skunk.

"Running scared, are you?" said Skunk. "Don't worry, I shan't hit you. I'll just walk around you three times."

"What balderdash." Black Hook was cross. "Go ahead and walk. I feel like taking a nap." Skunk twitched his whiskers. He picked up his pipe and filled it with some herbs from a tiny tobacco pouch.

"Wahli, kahli, woo woo," he whispered. Then he walked once around Black Hook, who was relaxing comfortably on the ground.

"Am I scaring you?" asked Skunk.

"Don't disturb me," Black Hook said dozily, as Skunk walked round him a second time.

"Scared now?" he asked.

"Not the teeniest little bit," came the reply.

"Onowani, Onowani, help me now," whispered Skunk. Instantly, a thick cloud of smoke poured out of his pipe and covered Black Hook. The evil spirit coughed and spluttered and choked. Worst of all was the horrible smell that filled his nose and clung to his furry skin. Black Hook rubbed his watering eyes with his hooks, but that horrible cloud of smoke would not go away.

"Oh, oh, what have you done," he screamed, "this smell is killing me!"

Skunk just stood calmly by. "Try cooling off in the river," he suggested at last.

Up jumped Black Hook. Coughing and spluttering, he hurled himself into the deep water. Well, he couldn't swim, could he? So that was the end of the evil spirit.

Skunk rushed off to tell the warriors and all the animals the good news that Black Hook was dead. But when he approached them, all the people and the animals ran away, for Onowani the Horrible came with him. And to this very day, Onowani stays with Skunk and helps him to escape from his enemies, as you'll find out if you ever get too close to him!

THE GOLDEN GOOSE

Grimm Brothers

In a faraway land many years ago there lived a couple who had three sons. The youngest boy was always teased by all the family for his foolish ways, and they nicknamed him "Dum Dum."

One day, the eldest son decided to go into the forest to chop some firewood. His mother packed a delicious meat pie and a bottle of cider to take with him. When lunchtime came, he sat down to eat, but he had just opened his bag when a little old man passed by and called, "Good day. Your food looks good. Will you give me a little piece of pie and a little of your cider, please? I am very hungry and thirsty."

"What? Give away some of my pie and my cider!" the eldest son said. "No, thank you. I wouldn't have enough for myself."

The little old man went away, and the young man, who thought he had dealt with the old man very cleverly, finished his lunch and went to chop up some logs. But he had just gotten started when his ax slipped. He cut his leg and had to limp home.

The next day, the second son decided he, too, would go into the forest to chop firewood.

His mother packed up a good dinner for him — a meat pie and a bottle of cider — and the second son set off. At noon, just as he was about to bite into his meat pie, the same little old man appeared again and asked for something to eat and drink. The second son called out rudely, "Whatever you get means I get less. Be off with you!"

The little old man walked away quietly, but no sooner had the second son started chopping again than his ax slipped, and he went home limping as well.

Then Dum Dum said, "Father, I'd like to go into the forest and chop wood, too."

"Your brothers have both hurt themselves," his father replied, "and you know nothing about axes, so you had better stay at home."

But Dum Dum begged so hard that at last his father said, "Go along, stupid. You'll soon learn your lesson if you're hurt."

Dum Dum set off into the forest, with only some dry bread and a bottle of sour milk, for his lunch, for that was all his mother had given him. When it was time to eat, the same little old man appeared before him. "Will you give me some meat and a little cider," he asked as before.

"I've only got dry bread and sour milk," Dum Dum said, "but you're welcome to share it if you like. Let us sit down and eat together."

So they sat down. When the boy unpacked his bread, he found that it had turned into a beautiful crusty pie, while the sour milk was now delicious cider. He and the little old man both ate and drank heartily, and when they had finished, the old man said, "You have a kind heart and have shared everything with me, so now I will give you something in return. Can you see that old tree? Cut it down and you'll find something worth having among its roots."

They shook hands, and the old man went away.

Dum Dum's ax did not slip, so before long he had cut down the tree. When it fell, lo and behold, a goose with feathers of pure gold was sitting in a hollow under the roots. Dum Dum picked up the

bird and said to himself, "I shan't go home to be laughed at. I shall go and seek my fortune."

So off he went, and some time later he came to an inn. Now the innkeeper had three daughters, and when they saw the golden goose, they were curious about the wonderful bird, and each wanted to have one of its beautiful golden feathers.

At last, the eldest said, "I *must* and *will* have a feather." She waited until Dum Dum turned his back, then she caught hold of the goose by the wing. But to her surprise, she couldn't pull her hand away.

Her second sister ran in to snatch a feather, too.

"I'm stuck," whispered the eldest sister, "pull me loose." But the moment the second sister touched her, she stuck fast as well.

The third sister came along, and the other two started screaming, "Keep back. For heaven's sake, keep back!"

But too late. The third sister was now stuck fast as well.

Soon Dum Dum picked up his goose and walked off, taking no notice of the three screaming girls. They had to follow, whether they liked it or not, for they were stuck fast. If Dum Dum ran, they had to run as well.

He led them across a rough field where they met a parson who was on his way to a church. He wagged a finger at the girls.

"Aren't you ashamed of yourselves, chasing after a young man like this? Is that good behavior?" And

he took hold of the youngest sister's hand to pull her away. The next moment, he was running along behind the little trail of people as well, for he too was stuck fast.

Presently the church elder came up, and he wondered why the parson was running after the three girls.

"Your Reverence," he said, "you're late for the service at the church." He pulled the parson's sleeve. And he stuck fast! There were now five people following Dum Dum.

Next they met two workers with pickaxes, and the parson shouted to them, "Help! Come and set us free!"

The workers tugged at the church elder and, of course, they stuck fast, too. This made seven people, all running after Dum Dum and his golden goose.

At last, they arrived at a big city. The city belonged to a king who had one daughter. Now, the princess never laughed or even smiled, and her father had proclaimed that whoever could make her laugh should have her for his wife.

As soon as Dum Dum heard this, he went to the palace with the goose under his arm, followed by the three innkeeper's daughters, the parson, the church elder and the two workers. When the princess saw the seven people hanging onto each other and treading on each other's heels, she thought they looked so funny that she couldn't help laughing. Dum Dum immediately claimed her for his wife. They were married the very next day and lived happily ever after.

Dum Dum wasn't quite such a dum-dum after all, was he?

THE ONE THAT
GOT AWAY

Jan Mark

"And what have we to remember to bring tomorrow?" Mrs. Cooper asked, at half past three. Malcolm, sitting near the back, wondered why she said "we." *She* wasn't going to bring anything.

"Something interesting, Mrs. Cooper," said everyone else, all together.

"And what are we going to do then?"

"Stand up and talk about it, Mrs. Cooper."

"So don't forget. All right. Chairs on tables. Goodbye, Class Four."

"Goodbye, Mrs. Cooper. Goodbye, everybody."

It all came out ever so slow, like saying the pledge in assembly. "Amen," said Malcolm, very quietly. Class Four put its chairs on the tables, collected its coats and went home, talking about all the interesting things it would bring into school tomorrow.

Malcolm walked by himself. Mrs. Cooper had first told them to find something interesting on Monday. Now it was Thursday, and still he had not come up with any bright ideas. There were plenty of things that he found interesting, but the trouble was, they never seemed to interest anyone else. Last time this had happened he had brought along his favorite stone and shown it to the class.

"Very nice, Malcolm," Mrs. Cooper had said. "Now tell us what's interesting about it." He hadn't known what to say. Surely anyone looking at the stone could see how interesting it was.

Mary was going to bring her gerbil. James, Sarah, and William had loudly discussed rare shells and fossils, and the only spider in the world with five legs.

"It can't be a spider then," said David, who was eavesdropping.

"It had an accident," William said.

Isobel intended to bring her pocket calculator and show them how it could write her name by punching in 738051 and turning it upside down. She did this every time, but it still looked interesting.

Malcolm could think of nothing.

When he reached home, he went up to his bedroom and looked at the shelf where he kept his important things; his twig that looked like a stick insect, his marble that looked like a glass eye, the penny with a hole in it, and the chewy,

delicious, candy slugs, one red and one green stuck together. He noticed that they were now stuck to the shelf, too. His stone had once been there as well, but after Class Four had said it was boring, he had put it back in the yard. He still went to see it sometimes.

What he really needed was something that could move around, like Mary's gerbil or William's five-legged spider. He sat down on his bed and began to think.

On Friday, after assembly, Class Four began to be interesting. Mary kicked off with the gerbil that whirred around its cage like a hairy balloon with the air escaping. Then they saw William's lame spider, James's fossil, Jason's collection of snail shells stuck one on top of the other like the Leaning Tower of Pisa, and David's bottled chestnuts that he had kept in an airtight jar for three years. They were still as glossy as new shoes.

71

Then it was Malcolm's turn. He went to the front and held out a matchbox. He had chosen it very carefully. It was the kind with the same label top and bottom, so that when you opened it, you could never be sure that it was the right way up and all the matches fell out. Malcolm opened it upside down and jumped. Mrs. Cooper jumped, too. Malcolm threw himself down on hands and knees and looked under her desk.

"What's the matter?" Mrs. Cooper said.

"It's fallen out!" Malcolm cried.

"What is it?" Mrs. Cooper said, edging away.

"I don't know – it's got six legs and sharp knees . . . and sort of frilly ginger eyebrows on stalks – " He pounced. "There it goes."

"Where?"

"Missed it," said Malcolm. "It's running under your chair, Mary."

Mary squeaked and climbed on to the table, because she thought that was the right way to behave when creepy-crawlies were about.

"I see it!" Jason yelled, and jumped up and

72

down. David threw a book in the direction that Jason was pointing, and James began beating the floor with a rolled-up comic.

"I got it – I killed it," he shouted.

"It's crawling up the curtains," Sarah said, and Mrs. Cooper, who was standing by the curtains, moved rapidly away from them.

"It's over by the door," Mary shrieked, and several people ran to head it off. Chairs were overturned.

Malcolm stood by Mrs. Cooper's desk with his matchbox. His contribution was definitely the most interesting thing that anyone had seen that morning. He was only sorry that he hadn't seen it himself.

TATTERCOATS

Joseph Jacobs

In a grand castle by the sea, there once lived a rich old nobleman. His only family was a granddaughter whose face he had never seen. He hated her bitterly because his favorite daughter had died when she was born. When the nurse showed him the newborn baby, he swore that it could live or die, he didn't care, and he vowed never to look on its face as long as he lived.

Then he turned his back and sat by his window looking out over the sea, weeping great tears for his dead daughter. His white hair and beard grew down over his shoulders as he sat, twining around his chair and creeping into the cracks in the floor. His tears, dropping on to the window ledge, wore away the stone and ran away in a river to the sea.

Meanwhile, his granddaughter grew up with no one to care for her. Only the old nurse, when no one was near, would give her a few scraps from the kitchen or a torn skirt from the ragbag. The other servants in the palace chased her outside with hard blows and cruel words. They called her "Tattercoats" and laughed at her bare feet and her ragged clothes until she ran away to cry and hide among the bushes.

And so she grew up, having little to eat or wear. She spent her days in the fields, with only the gooseherd to keep her company. But he could play to her so merrily on his pipe whenever she was hungry, cold, or tired, that she forgot all her troubles and would start dancing, with his flock of noisy geese for her partners.

One day, news came that the king was traveling through the country and that he was giving a great ball in the town. All the lords and ladies were to be invited because his only son, the prince, was to choose a bride.

An invitation was taken to the castle by the sea, and the servants took it up to the old lord who was still

sitting by the window, wrapped in his long white hair and weeping into the little river.

But when he received the king's invitation, he dried his eyes and ordered his servants to bring some shears to cut him loose, for his long hair and beard had made him a prisoner in his chair and he could not move. Then he sent for rich clothes and jewels and, when he had put them on, he ordered them to saddle his favorite white horse so that he might ride out to greet the king.

Of course, Tattercoats heard all about the exciting events in the nearby town, and she sat by the kitchen door crying sadly because she could not join in. When the old nurse heard her weeping, she went to the lord of the castle and begged him to take his granddaughter with him to the king's ball. But he only frowned and scowled.

"Be silent, woman," he shouted; and the servants all laughed and said, "Tattercoats is happy in her rags, chattering and dancing with the gooseherd. That's all she's good for. Leave her alone!"

The old nurse begged once, twice, three times more. "Let your granddaughter go with you." But her only answer was a black look and angry words, and at last the servants drove her out of the room.

Sadly and sorrowfully, the old nurse went to look for Tattercoats, but the girl had heard the rough words spoken to the nurse and had already run away to her friend, the gooseherd.

"Alas, my grandfather still hates me and will not take me to the ball," she told him.

The gooseherd listened thoughtfully. "Never mind, Tattercoats. We shall go to the town and see the king and all the fine clothes anyway." Tattercoats looked unhappily at her ragged skirt and her cold bare feet, but the gooseherd played a few merry notes on his pipe, and she soon forgot all her worries and laughed away her tears. Before she knew what was happening, he took her by the hand, and he and she set off dancing along the road with the cackling geese in front of them.

As they were dancing along, a young man dressed in wonderful clothes rode up to them and asked if they could show him the way to the castle where the king was staying. When they told him that they were going that way, too, he got down from his horse and walked along beside them.

The gooseherd kept on playing, but now the tunes were low and soft and sweet. The young man could not take his eyes off Tattercoats' beautiful face and soon he had fallen in love with her. "Marry me," he begged.

Tattercoats shook her golden hair and smiled gently. "It would be shameful for you to marry an unknown beggar-girl," she said. "Go and find a wife among the ladies you will meet at the king's ball. Do not mock my rags or my name of Tattercoats."

The piper played more sweetly, she refused the young man more kindly, and he fell in love more deeply. At last, he begged her to come to the ball.

"Come just as you are now," he said. "Come in your rags with your bare feet. Come with the gooseherd and his geese, and I will dance with you before the king and all his lords and ladies. I will tell them you are to be my dearest wife." And he leaped upon his horse and rode away.

That night, the grand hall in the castle was filled with music and everyone was dancing in front of the king. As the clock struck twelve, the great doors were flung open, and Tattercoats, the gooseherd, and the flock of noisy cackling geese walked calmly in. How the grand ladies giggled and the lords all whispered and laughed! The king, sitting on his splendid throne, stared in astonishment, but when Tattercoats reached the throne, the prince himself stepped forward. He took Tattercoats' hand and kissed her gently three times. Then he turned to the king and bowed.

"Father," he said, "I have found the loveliest, sweetest girl in all the land to be my bride. Tattercoats is my choice."

As he spoke, the gooseherd started to play a soft, sweet tune and Tattercoats' rags fell away and she stood dressed in shining robes covered with glittering jewels. A glistening crown appeared on her golden hair, and the cackling geese turned into young pages to carry her long silken train.

Then the king rose to meet his son's bride and ordered the trumpets to sound in her honor, and the people rejoiced that the prince had chosen his bride. But the gooseherd disappeared and was never seen again.

As for the old lord, he went back to his empty castle by the sea, for even now he would not look on his granddaughter's face. He still sits by his window, weeping and weeping as he looks out across the sea, a bitter and lonely old man.

PO-WAN AND KUAN-YIN

A Chinese traditional tale

In China, many years ago, a boy was born into the family of Chin, which means gold. He was named Po-wan, which means a million, because it was foretold that one day he would be rich and have a million pieces of gold.

But Po-wan spent all his money on the poor. He gave away so much that he hardly had any food for himself, and his clothes were always worn and ragged.

One day, he asked himself, "Why is it that I, who am called A Million Pieces of Gold, have not a penny to give a beggar or a bowl of rice to share with him?" He decided to go and seek the answer from the wise goddess, Kuan-yin.

Po-wan traveled for many days until he came to a wide and fast-flowing river. As he stood on the river-bank deciding how he could cross, a deep voice called from the hilltop, "Po-wan, are you going to see Kuan-yin?"

"Yes," replied Po-wan, wondering who was calling to him.

"Then would you ask her a question for me?"

Po-wan knew that he could ask Kuan-yin only three questions, but, as he had only one of his own to ask, he willingly agreed to the voice's request.

Then a huge snake appeared over the hill. It was so enormous it could easily have swallowed Po-wan up in one gulp. Po-wan trembled with fear.

"Ask Kuan-yin why it is that, although I am a thousand and one years old, I am not yet a dragon," hissed the snake. "For I am good and never greedy, as you can see."

Po-wan was very relieved to hear this.

"I will ask her," he said. "But how am I to cross this river?"

"I shall take you on my back," declared the snake.

Po-wan hung on tightly to the snake's slippery back and was very glad to reach the other side. He hurried on his way and soon came to an inn where he asked for a bowl of rice.

"What brings you here?" asked the innkeeper.

Po-wan told him that he was on his way to visit Kuan-yin.

"Then ask her a question for me," pleaded the innkeeper. "My beautiful daughter cannot speak. Please ask Kuan-yin why this is so."

Po-wan felt sorry for the innkeeper and readily agreed. After all, Kuan-yin would answer three questions, and Po-wan had only one of his own.

Po-wan traveled on until it was dark. At the next house he came to, he asked if he could have a bed for the night. The house belonged to a rich man who gave Po-wan a good meal and a comfortable bed to sleep in.

Next morning, when Po-wan was about to leave, the rich man called out, "As you are going to Kuan-yin, would you ask her a question for

me? In my garden are many special plants and trees
that have been well looked after for twenty years.
But none of them will flower or bear fruit. Please
ask Kuan-yin why this is so."

"Of course I will," promised Po-wan without
hesitation.

Alas! He was allowed to ask Kuan-yin only
three questions, and now there were four. What
should he do?

Po-wan knew the answer.

"I have made promises to the Great Snake, the
innkeeper and the rich man," he said to himself,
"and promises must be kept."

When Po-wan arrived at Kuan-yin's temple,
she invited him to ask his three questions.

"Why is the Great Snake not yet a dragon when he has been good and never greedy for a thousand and one years?"

Kuan-yin replied, "There are seven pearls on his head. Only if he takes six away will he become a dragon."

Next, Po-wan asked, "Why can the innkeeper's daughter not speak?"

Kuan-yin replied, "It will be so until she sees the man she will marry."

Then Po-wan asked, "Why are there no flowers or fruit in the rich man's garden?"

Kuan-yin replied, "There are seven caskets of gold and silver in his garden. There will be no flowers nor fruit until he gives away half this treasure."

Po-wan thanked Kuan-yin and set off home. First, he gave the rich man the goddess' answer. The rich man was so grateful that he gave Po-wan half his treasure. Next, Po-wan went to the innkeeper to tell him what Kuan-yin had said. When the innkeeper's daughter saw him from her open window, she called out, "Welcome back, Po-wan!"

The innkeeper was so delighted to hear his daughter speak, he agreed at once to let her marry Po-wan.

Then Po-wan went to the Great Snake and told him what the goddess had said. The snake gave six of his pearls to Po-wan and was immediately transformed into a magnificent dragon.

And that is how Chin Po-wan, through his kindness and goodness, came to be a rich man worth a million gold pieces.

NUMBER TWELVE

Leila Berg

One day, twelve people went fishing. All friends.

There was Mandy and Sandy, and Jimmy and Timmy. That makes four. There was Poll and Moll, and Ted and Ned. That makes eight. And Bobby and Robby is ten, and Lindy and Cindy is twelve . . . I *think*.

Hm, let me count them again. There was Lindy and Cindy and Bobby and Robby. That makes four. And Poll and Moll and Ted and Ned. That makes eight. And Mandy and Timmy is ten, and Sandy and Jimmy is twelve . . . I *think*.

Well, anyway, they all went fishing. And the sun shone, and the water of the river winked and flashed in the sun. Oh, it was a glorious day for fishing!

Mandy caught a piece of wood.
Timmy caught a sausage can.
Jimmy caught a boot.
Moll caught Cindy.
Poll caught a tree.
Ned caught the other side.
Cindy caught a man in a boat.
Ted caught Sandy.
Bobby caught a fantastic hat.
Robby caught a buggy wheel.
Lindy caught Sandy.
Sandy caught herself.
Everyone caught something,
so they were all very happy.
They went home talking and
shouting and singing.
"I caught a shark in the sea!"
"I caught a thousand sharks!"
"I caught a whale in the sea!"
"I caught a million whales!"
"An octopus strangled me!"
"I strangled an octopus!"

"I'm Superman!"

"I'm Superwoman!"

"I nearly drowned!"

"*I* nearly drowned!"

"*We* nearly drowned *millions* of times!"

"How do you know if someone has drowned?" said Lindy.

"You just count," said Ned, "and if you're one short, then you know someone has drowned."

They thought they had better make sure that no one had drowned. So they all got in a long line, and Ned stood in front of them and walked down the line, counting.

"Lindy is one, Cindy is two, Mandy is three, Sandy is four, Jimmy is five, Timmy is six, Robby is seven, Bobby is eight, Poll is nine, Moll is ten, Ted is eleven, and . . ."

There was no one else there! Only eleven people! But there were twelve when they went out to fish.

They began to run about, looking for Number Twelve.

"Where are you, Number Twelve? Where are you?" But nobody answered.

After a bit, Poll said, "Make a line again. I'll count."

So they made a line again, and Poll counted.

"Ned is one and Ted is two. Sandy is three and Mandy is four. Jimmy is five and Timmy is six. Lindy is seven and Cindy is eight. Bobby is nine and Robby is ten. Moll is eleven and . . ."

There was no one else to count. Number Twelve had gone!

They were really scared. They ran about looking for Number Twelve. Somebody else counted, and then somebody else. But whoever counted – and in the end, *everybody* had a turn at counting – it always came to the same, eleven. No Number Twelve. But they certainly had Number Twelve when they started out.

"Somebody's drowned!" they cried to each other. "Somebody's drowned!"

And they all ran back to the river and ran along the bank, looking and calling and looking and

calling, and back the way they came, looking and calling again.

But not a sign did they see of Number Twelve. So they began to cry, all of them.

While they were sitting in a heap, crying, a man came along.

"Whatever's the matter?" he said.

"We've lost Number Twelve, poor Number Twelve! Number Twelve's drowned," they wailed.

"Really? Why do you say that?"

"We counted. We all counted. But there's no Number Twelve any more."

"Now calm down," he said (for the noise was tremendous). "Just count again for me."

So Cindy counted. Everyone got in a line, and Cindy walked along it, counting. And it came to eleven.

"Yes, you're right," said the man. "I see. I shall have to think very hard about this. You're rather lucky I came along, you know. I *think*, I really do *think*, that I *might* be able to find Number Twelve for you. But what will you give me if I do?"

"Oh, everything we've got, everything!" And they emptied their pockets on the spot and gave him everything that was in them. They did want to see dear Number Twelve again.

"Right!" said the man. "Stand in a line, everyone."

And he took a stick and counted each one of them, and tapped each head with the stick as he counted.

"There's one. There's two. There's three. There's four. There's five. There's six. There's seven. There's eight. There's nine. There's ten. There's eleven."

And when he got to twelve – because of course there *were* twelve of them when they were all together in one line – he gave that one an extra hard bonk on the head.

"THERE'S NUMBER TWELVE!" he shouted.

They were so excited! So pleased! So thankful! They all rushed up to Number Twelve.

"You're back! How lovely to see you! We thought we'd never find you again! Let me give you a hug! Let me give you a kiss! Where have you *been*?" Then they all, all of them, shouted together, "Yes, where have you *been*?"

And Number Twelve, who was still quite dazed from the thump, said, "Me? I don't think I've been anywhere."

"Don't be so silly. You *must* have been some- where or we couldn't have found you," they said. "Wasn't it lucky we did?"

And they all went home, the twelve of them . . . Or eleven . . . Or was it thirteen? . . . Hm.

THE HUSBAND
WHO LOOKED
AFTER THE HOUSE

A Scandinavian traditional tale

O nce upon a time, a man called Peter and his wife Hana lived together in a cottage. Peter worked hard on their farm: plowing the fields, sowing the crops, and gathering them in at harvest time. Hana also worked hard: looking after their cow, milking her and churning the cream into butter, cleaning the house, and cooking their food. The two were happy enough, except that Peter always thought that he worked harder than his wife.

"If only I could sit in the shade and churn a little cream into butter instead of cutting the hay in the meadow," he said, shaking his head. "You have an easy time of it, wife."

"It's none so easy," replied Hana. "Why don't we swap jobs tomorrow and then you'll see. I'll work in the fields, and you can stay at home and look after things here." Peter thought this was an excellent idea.

Early next morning, Hana set off to the meadow with her scythe, while Peter stayed at home.

First, he decided to churn the cream into butter. He hadn't been churning for long when he began to feel thirsty. A nice mug of beer was what he needed, he decided, so he went down to the cellar. He had just turned the tap on the beer barrel when he heard a terrible noise upstairs in the kitchen. He rushed up the steps, and what a sight met his eyes! There in the kitchen was the pig. It had come in from the yard, knocked over the churn, and was now guzzling up the cream.

Peter shouted at the pig and gave it such a kick that it flew out of the door into the yard. Then he remembered his beer. He ran back down the cellar steps. But he was too late! Every last drop of beer had run out of the barrel onto the cellar floor.

Peter had to start all over again. He filled the churn with cream and churned away for a while. But then he remembered that the cow was still shut in the barn. She had not eaten a blade of grass or had a drop of water all morning.

"It'll take me an hour to take her up to the field and come home again," he thought. "While I'm gone, the butter will spoil in the churn. What shall I do?"

"I know," he said. "I'll take her up on to the roof."

(This may sound strange, but in that country, the roofs of some houses were covered with grass, not shingles.) Peter's house stood close to a steep hill, and he decided to lay a plank from the hill to the roof and lead the cow across.

He didn't dare leave the churn this time, so he loaded it on to his back before setting off to the barn. On his way, Peter remembered that the cow had not had a drink. So he grabbed a bucket and went to the well. But, as he leaned over, all the cream ran out of the churn, over his shoulders, and down into the well.

"Oh dear!" shouted Peter. "What shall I do? It's nearly lunchtime, and I haven't even churned the

butter yet. I'd better make some soup for lunch and
churn the butter later."

So he went back to the kitchen and set a pot of
water on the fire. Then he remembered the cow.

"She still hasn't had anything to eat or drink,
poor thing," he cried.

This time, he got the water safely from the well
and took it to the barn. The cow was indeed very
thirsty, and she quickly drank the bucket dry.

Then Peter led her up on to the roof. As soon as
he got there, he began to worry about the water on
the fire. He ran down to the kitchen, but all was
well. Quickly, Peter cut up some carrots and some
onions and threw them into the pot.

Just as he had finished, he began to worry about
the cow.

"What if she falls off the roof and breaks her leg?" he thought. "I'd better tie her up."

So he found a length of rope and went back on to the roof. Peter tied one end of the rope around the cow's neck, but there was nowhere to tie the other end. Then he had a brilliant idea. He slipped the end of the rope down the chimney, ran back down into the kitchen, and tied the rope round his leg. "That will keep her safe," he said, feeling very pleased with himself.

Now the soup was beginning to smell good. Peter stirred the onions and carrots, and looked around for some beans to add to them. But just at that moment, the cow slipped and fell off the roof. As she fell, her weight dragged Peter halfway up the chimney. And there he stuck fast!

Out in the meadow, Peter's wife decided she had waited long enough for her lunch, so she set off for home. What a sight met her eyes! There was the poor cow swinging from the roof on a rope. Quick as a flash, she raised her scythe and cut through the rope. The cow landed softly on a pile of hay.

But inside the house, there was a terrible crash. Peter's wife rushed into the kitchen. And what did she see? With the cow's weight gone from the rope, Peter had come tumbling down the chimney. There he was, upside down, in the soup kettle!

"Well, that's a funny way to cook," said his wife as she hauled him out.

"Oh, Hana," cried Peter. "You were right. This work of yours is none so easy!"

"You'll soon get used to it," she replied.

"Oh, no," cried Peter. "Please let me go back to my work in the fields, and I promise that I will never say that I work harder than you again!"

Hana smiled and nodded her head. After that the two of them lived together in peace for the rest of their lives.

SLEEPING BEAUTY

Charles Perrault

Once upon a time, there lived a king and queen who longed for children, but had none. One day, while the queen was bathing, a frog hopped out of the water and said, "Your wish will be granted, and you shall have a beautiful baby daughter." The king and queen were both delighted.

When the time came and their baby was born, the king gave a great feast for her christening, and hundreds of guests were invited. The king also invited all the fairies in the kingdom – all the fairies, that is, except one, for there were thirteen fairies in all, and the king only had twelve gold plates.

All the guests at the feast agreed that the princess was the most beautiful baby they had ever seen. Soon it was time for each of the fairies to present their gifts to the princess. The first fairy gave her the gift of goodness, the second beauty, the third riches, and so on until all but the twelfth fairy had stepped forward.

But just as the twelfth fairy approached the cradle, there was the sound of rushing wind, and the doors of the great hall flew open. There stood

the thirteenth fairy, and she was furious that she had not been invited.

"Beauty and riches the princess may have," she cackled, "but on her sixteenth birthday, she will

prick her finger on a spindle and fall down dead."
With that, she swept out of the room, and a terrible
hush fell over the guests.

But the twelfth fairy had still to make her wish.
She couldn't undo the terrible spell, but she could
soften it.

"The princess will not die," she said. "Instead,
she will fall into a deep sleep that will last for one
hundred years."

The king and queen were overcome with grief
and the king immediately ordered all the spindles in
the kingdom to be burned.

The years passed, and the princess grew into the
happiest, kindest, and most beautiful child anyone
had ever seen. It seemed as though all the wishes of
the first eleven fairies had come true.

At last, the time came for the princess to
celebrate her sixteenth birthday, and the king and
queen held a great ball for her in the palace. People
came from far and wide to the grand birthday
ball, where a magnificent banquet was laid out.
After all the guests had eaten and drunk as much
as they could and danced until their feet were
sore, the princess asked if they could all play a
game of hide-and-seek. It was agreed that the
princess should be the first to hide, and she
quickly sped away.

The princess ran to a far corner of the palace and
found herself climbing a spiral staircase in a turret
she did not remember ever visiting before.

"They will never find me
here," she thought as she crept
into a little room at the top. But, to her surprise,
she found an old woman dressed in black sitting on
a chair, spinning.

"What are you doing?" questioned the princess
as she saw the spindle twirling, for she had never
seen anything like it in her whole life.

"Come and see, my pretty," replied the old
woman. The princess watched fascinated as the
old woman pulled the strands of wool, twirling
them into one thread with her fingers and
feeding it onto the spindle.

"Would you like to try?" she asked cunningly.

The princess sat down and took the spindle in
her hands. No sooner had she done so than she
pricked her thumb and fell down as though dead.
The wicked fairy's spell had worked!

But the princess did not die. The twelfth fairy's wish also came true and instead the princess fell into a deep, deep sleep.

The spell worked upon everyone else in the palace, too. The king and queen fell asleep in their thrones. The guests dropped off to sleep where they stood. In the kitchen, the cook fell asleep as she was about to box the scullery boy's ears, and the scullery maid nodded off as she was plucking a chicken. The meat on the fire stopped roasting, and even the flies on the wall stopped their buzzing. All over the palace, a great silence descended.

A thick hedge of thorns sprang up around the palace until it was completely hidden from view. As the years passed, people sometimes asked what

lay behind the hedge, but few now remembered the palace where the king and queen had lived with their lovely daughter. Sometimes curious travelers tried to force their way through, but the hedge grew so thick that they soon gave up.

One day, many many years later, a prince came riding by. He asked, like other travelers, what lay behind the thorn hedge. An old man told him a story he had heard about a palace behind the thorns and a beautiful princess who lay asleep for one hundred years. The prince became curious and decided to cut his way through the thorns. But when he came to the thorn hedge, it seemed to open out before his sword, and in a short while the prince was inside the grounds. He ran across the gardens and through an open door into the lovely old palace.

Everywhere he looked – in the great hall, in the kitchens, in the corridors and on the staircases – he saw people asleep. He passed through many rooms until he found himself climbing a winding staircase in an old turret. There, in a small room at the top, he found himself staring in wonder at the most beautiful girl he had ever seen. She was so lovely, that, without thinking, he leaned forward and gently kissed her.

As his lips touched hers, the princess began to stir, and she opened her eyes. The first thing she saw was a handsome young man. As she gazed up at him, she fell deeply in love.

The prince and princess came down the turret stairs together and found the whole castle coming back to life. In the great hall, the king and queen were stretching and yawning, puzzled over how they could have dropped off to sleep during their daughter's party. Their guests, too, were shaking their heads, rubbing their eyes, and wondering why they felt so sleepy. In the kitchen, the cook boxed the scullery boy's ears, and the scullery maid carried on plucking the chicken. The meat started to roast again, and the flies to buzz around. The hundred-year spell had been broken.

The princess told her parents how much she loved the handsome young man who had kissed her, and they were delighted to find he was a prince from a neighboring country. The king gave the couple his blessing, and a grand wedding was arranged.

At the wedding party, the princess looked more beautiful than ever, and the prince loved her more with every moment. The twelve good fairies who had come to her christening were invited once again and were delighted to see the happiness of the prince and princess. Toward evening the newly married pair rode off together to their new home in the prince's country, where they lived happily ever after.

MR. PEPPERPOT
BUYS MACARONI

Alf Prøysen

*Mrs Pepperpot is just an ordinary old lady, except that
she sometimes shrinks to the size of a pepperpot . . .*

"It's been a very long time since we had macaroni
for supper," said Mr. Pepperpot one day.

"Then you shall have it today, my love," said
his wife. "But I shall have to go to the grocer for
some. So first of all you'll have to find me."

"Find you?" said Mr. Pepperpot. "What sort of
nonsense is that?" But when he looked around for
her, he couldn't see her anywhere. "Don't be silly,
wife," he said; "if you're hiding in the cupboard,
you must come out this minute. We're too big to
play hide-and-seek."

"*I'm* not too big, I'm just the right size for
'hunt-the-pepperpot'," laughed Mrs. Pepperpot.
"Find me if you can!"

"I'm not going to charge around my own
bedroom looking for my wife," he said crossly.

"Now, now! I'll help you; I'll tell you when you're warm. Just now you're very cold." For Mr. Pepperpot was peering out of the window, thinking she might have jumped out. As he searched around the room, she called out, "Warm!", "Colder!", "Getting hotter!" until he was quite dizzy.

At last she shouted, "You'll burn the top of your bald head if you don't look up!" And there she was, sitting on the bedpost, swinging her legs and laughing at him.

Her husband made a very long face when he saw her. "This is a bad business — a very bad business," he said, stroking her cheek with his little finger.

"I don't think it's a bad business," said Mrs. Pepperpot.

"I shall have a terrible time. The whole town will laugh when they see I have a wife the size of a pepperpot."

"Who cares?" she answered. "That doesn't

matter a bit. Now put me down on the floor so that I can get ready to go to the grocery store and buy your macaroni."

But her husband wouldn't hear of her going; he would go to the grocery himself.

"That'll be a lot of use!" she said. "When you get home, you'll have forgotten to buy the macaroni. I'm sure even if I wrote 'macaroni' right across your forehead, you'd bring back cinnamon and salted herrings instead."

"But how are you going to walk all that way with those tiny legs?"

"Put me in your coat pocket; then I won't need to walk."

There was no help for it, so Mr. Pepperpot put his wife in his pocket and set off for the store.

Soon she started talking, "My goodness me, what a lot of strange things you have in your pocket — screws and nails, tobacco and matches — there's even a fishhook! You'll have to take that out at once; I might get it caught in my skirt."

"Don't talk so loud," said her husband, as he took out the fishhook. "We're going into the store now."

It was an old-fashioned store where they sold everything from prunes to coffee cups. The grocer was particularly proud of the coffee cups and held one up, for Mr. Pepperpot to see. This made his wife curious, and she popped her head out of his pocket.

"You stay where you are!" whispered Mr. Pepperpot.

"I beg your pardon, did you say something?" asked the grocer.

"No, no, I was just humming a little tune," said Mr Pepperpot. "Tra-la-la!"

"What color are the cups?" whispered his wife. And her husband sang:

"The cups are blue
With gold edge, too,
But they cost too much
So that won't do!"

After that, Mrs. Pepperpot kept quiet — but not for long. When her husband pulled out his tobacco she couldn't resist hanging on to the lid. Neither her husband nor anyone else in the shop noticed her slipping onto the counter and hiding behind a

flour bag. From there, she darted silently across to the scales, crawled under them, past a pair of smoked mackerel wrapped in paper, and found herself next to the coffee cups.

"Aren't they pretty!" she whispered, and took a step backward to get a better view. Whoops! She fell right into the macaroni drawer, which had been left open. She hastily covered herself up with macaroni, but the grocer heard the scratching noise and quickly banged the drawer shut. You see, it did sometimes happen that mice got into the drawers, and that's not the sort of thing you want people to know about, so the grocer pretended nothing had happened and went on waiting on people.

There was Mrs. Pepperpot all in the dark; she could hear the grocer waiting on her husband now.

"That's good," she thought. "When he orders macaroni I'll get my chance to slip into the bag with it."

But it was just as she had feared; her husband
forgot what he had come to buy. Mrs. Pepperpot
shouted at the top of her voice, "MACARONI!",
but it was impossible to get him to hear.

"A quarter of a pound of coffee, please," said
her husband.

"Anything else?" asked the grocer.

"MACARONI!" shouted Mrs. Pepperpot.

"Two pounds of sugar," said her husband.

"Anything more?"

"MACARONI!" shouted Mrs. Pepperpot.

But at last, her husband remembered the
macaroni of his own accord. The grocer hurriedly
filled a bag. He thought he felt something move,
but he didn't say a word.

"That's all, thank you," said Mr. Pepperpot.
When he got outside the door, he was just about
to make sure his wife was still in his pocket when a
van drew up and offered to give him a ride all the
way home. Once there, he took off his knapsack

with all the shopping in it and put his hand in his pocket to lift out his wife.

The pocket was empty.

Now he was really frightened. First he thought she was teasing him, but when he had called three times and still no wife appeared, he put on his hat again and hurried back to the store.

The grocer saw him coming. "He's probably going to complain about the mouse in the macaroni," he thought.

"Have you forgotten anything, Mr. Pepperpot?" he asked, and smiled as pleasantly as he could.

Mr. Pepperpot was looking all round. "Yes," he said.

"I would be very grateful, Mr. Pepperpot, if you would keep it to yourself about the mouse being in the macaroni. I'll let you have these fine blue coffee cups if you'll say no more about it."

"Mouse?" Mr. Pepperpot looked puzzled.

"Shh!" said the grocer, and hurriedly started wrapping up the cups.

Then Mr. Pepperpot realized that the grocer had mistaken his wife for a mouse. So he took the cups and rushed home as fast as he could. By the time he got there, he was in a sweat of fear that his wife might have been squeezed to death in the macaroni bag.

"Oh, my dear wife," he muttered to himself. "My poor darling wife. I'll never again be ashamed of you being the size of a pepperpot – as long as you're still alive!"

When he opened the door, she was standing by the cooking-stove, dishing up the macaroni – as large as life; in fact, as large as you or I.

RED UMBRELLA
AND
YELLOW SCARF

Anita Hewett

Monkey put on his yellow scarf.

"It is warm today," said Marmoset. "That yellow scarf is useless, Monkey."

Monkey opened his red umbrella and held it high above his head.

"It is dry today," said Marmoset. "That red umbrella is useless, Monkey."

Monkey did not say a word. He smiled and walked away through the jungle, his yellow scarf around his neck, his red umbrella above his head.

He came to a stream and saw Jacana. Jacana Bird stepped along on the bank, and her five little chicks bobbed and scuttled behind her, black and golden, like bumblebees.

Mother Jacana turned her head, fluttering yellow wings at the chicks.

"Now we must cross the stream," she said. "You are far too fluffy and small for swimming. Here is a pathway of lily pad leaves. Walk carefully, chicks. The water is deep."

The shiny round leaves lay still on the water, making a pathway from bank to bank. Jacana stepped on a lily pad, spreading out her long, thin toes.

"Come," she called. "This leaf is safe."

The five little chicks hopped on the leaf, and cheeped as it dipped and swayed beneath them.

Mother Jacana stepped to the next leaf.

"Come," she called. "This leaf is safe." And the five little chicks scuttled behind her.

Now they were halfway across the stream.

"Come," called Mother Jacana again.

Four little chicks scuttled behind her. The last one stood still, looking at a lily bud.

"Why have you closed yourself up?" he asked. "What are you hiding inside you, lily bud?"

He pushed his beak between the petals and wriggled his head inside the bud. And he found himself staring into the eyes of the biggest brown bee he had ever seen.

"Buzz!" went the bee. The chick fell backward and slid across the lily pad, splashing in the stream among the little silver bubbles.

Monkey did not have a boat. But he had his scarf, and he had his umbrella. He turned the umbrella upside down, so that it floated on the water. He tied on the yellow scarf for a sail. Then he sat in his red umbrella-boat and sailed down the stream to Jacana Chick. He lifted him gently out of the water and set him down on the lily pad. Jacana

Chick jumped up and down on the leaf, shaking the water out of his fluff. Then he bobbed and scuttled after his mother. When Mother Jacana turned round, there were five little chicks on the leaf behind her.

"Come," she said. "We have reached the bank."

Monkey walked away from the stream, his yellow scarf around his neck, his red umbrella above his head. He came to a cliff and sat down to rest. He heard a little snuffling sound and leaned out over the cliff to look. A soft, round, golden-brown creature was clinging to a creeper vine. She lifted her small furry face to Monkey, staring with unhappy eyes.

"Be careful, Little Opossum," called Monkey. "Don't fall onto those rocks below."

Little Opossum started to climb, clinging tightly with her claws, moving up and up the creeper until she was close to the top of the cliff. Monkey stretched out a paw to help her.

Snap! The creeper broke in half!

"Oh-ee-ee!" cried Little Opossum. Down she fell to the rocks below.

Monkey did not have a ladder. But he had his scarf, and he had his umbrella. He turned the umbrella upside down and tied it to the yellow scarf. Then he lay on the grass at the edge of the cliff and gently lowered the red umbrella until it rested beside Little Opossum.

Little Opossum sat in the umbrella. It rocked as
Monkey pulled it up, and Little Opossum hid her
face in her paws.

"You are safe," said Monkey. "Open your eyes."

Little Opossum climbed from the umbrella and
trotted happily over the grass.

Monkey walked away from the cliff, his yellow
scarf around his neck, his red umbrella above his
head. He went to the mud flats and sat on a shell
bank. He shaded his eyes from the sun with his paw
and looked across the mangrove trees standing on
tangled roots in the mud. Among the roots sat

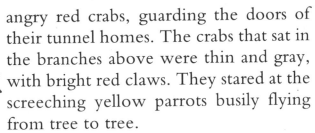

angry red crabs, guarding the doors of their tunnel homes. The crabs that sat in the branches above were thin and gray, with bright red claws. They stared at the screeching yellow parrots busily flying from tree to tree.

Then Monkey saw Turtle. Poor old Turtle was trying to find his way to the shell bank. He was old and tired, and he seemed to be lost as he plodded along by the mangrove trees.

"Keep away, keep away!" called the angry red crabs.

"Get out, get out!" screamed the thin gray crabs.

"Chase him away!" screeched the yellow parrots.

Turtle did not know where to turn.

"This way, Turtle," Monkey called.

Turtle turned toward the shell bank. The angry red crabs, the thin gray crabs, and the screeching

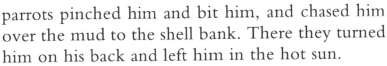

parrots pinched him and bit him, and chased him over the mud to the shell bank. There they turned him on his back and left him in the hot sun.

"Poor old Turtle," Monkey said. He put out a paw and lifted old Turtle, setting him gently onto his legs. But Turtle could not move away. The sun was too hot, and his feet were too sore. He wanted to sleep until he felt better.

Monkey did not have a bed. But he had his scarf, and he had his umbrella.

He folded the scarf to make a bed and stood the umbrella beside it, for shade. Then he lifted poor old Turtle again and put him down on the yellow bed. Turtle sighed and closed his eyes.

When the sun went down behind the mangroves, Turtle smiled and stretched his legs. Then he stumped away happily home to his supper.

"And I must go home to *my* supper," said Monkey.

He smiled to himself as he walked away, his yellow scarf around his neck, his red umbrella above his head.

As soon as he reached his tree in the jungle, he took off his scarf and folded it neatly.

"It was warm today," said Marmoset. "That yellow scarf was useless, Monkey."

Monkey closed the red umbrella and hung it carefully over a branch.

"It was dry today," said Marmoset. "That red umbrella was useless, Monkey."

Monkey did not say a word. Later, perhaps, he would tell Marmoset. But now it was time for his supper.

MOLLIE WHUPPIE

*An English tale
retold by Susan Price*

Once upon a time, there were three sisters. Two of the sisters were tall, beautiful girls, but the youngest was small and mischievous. Her name was Mollie Whuppie.

One dark night, the three sisters got lost in a wood, and they had to knock on the door of a strange house to ask for shelter.

"Come you in," said the woman who answered the door. "Sit you down." And she made her own three daughters get down from the table, and then she fed Mollie and her sisters until their bellies were stretched tight.

Now the woman's husband was a giant, and when he came home, he said, "I smell the blood of English lasses."

"There are three," his wife told him. "They'll sleep with ours tonight."

But before they all went to bed, the giant called his three daughters to him and tied a soft silken ribbon around each of their necks. Around the necks of Mollie and her sisters, he tied harsh ropes of straw. Then his wife took all six into the next room and tucked them into a big bed.

"Sleep well," she said.

They soon slept – except Mollie Whuppie. From the next room she heard the giant say, "Light the fire, wife. Make the oven hot. I shall kill the geese."

Quick as a flash, Mollie took the silken ribbons from the necks of the giant's daughters and tied them around her own and her sisters' necks. The harsh straw ropes she tied around the necks of the three young giantesses.

The door of the bedroom creaked, and then it opened, and in tiptoed the giant. He came to the bed and, in the darkness, felt for the girls' necks. Each time he felt a rough straw rope, he lifted that girl out of the bed and laid her on the floor. But the girls wearing silken ribbons he left in the bed, thinking they were his daughters.

Then he picked up the three girls on the floor, ran outside, and threw them into a deep chasm.

"Come down, I'll fetch these fat geese for the oven," growled the giant.

As soon as the giant had gone, Mollie woke her sisters and they climbed out of the window and ran away. They ran until they came to the deep chasm, and the only bridge across was the edge of a sharp sword blade.

"We'll be cut to pieces!" said the two sisters, but Mollie said, "Run lightly and have courage," and she led her sisters across.

On the other side was the king's palace, and they went there and told him their tale.

"You have done well, Mollie Whuppie," said the king, "but you can do better. Did you see the giant's bow?"

"It hung on the wall behind his chair," said Mollie Whuppie.

"An arrow from that bow never misses," said the king. "Steal it for me and I'll marry my eldest son to your eldest sister, and she'll never want for anything again."

"Done!" said Mollie, and she washed her face, changed her clothes, and combed her hair so that she looked unlike herself. Then, although her sisters begged her not to go, she ran lightly across Sword Bridge and into the forest.

It was already dark when she got to the giant's house. She knocked and asked for lodgings, and the giant's wife didn't know her, but let her in. The giant was at the table, counting gold from a purse. Behind him hung the beautiful bow.

Mollie sat by the fire until the giant's wife went to make her bed. She saw the giant hide his purse under his pillow before he went to get more logs for the fire. Quick as a flash, Mollie snatched the bow from the wall and ran from the house. But the bow shouted out, "Help! Help!" and the giant heard.

Mollie ran and the giant ran after, knocking down trees as he went. But Mollie reached Sword Bridge first and lightly crossed it. The giant was afraid to follow, the bridge being so sharp and him so heavy.

"Pain to you, Mollie Whuppie! Never come again!"

"Twice more," she said, "twice more."

She gave the bow to the king, and her eldest sister was married to the eldest prince, and the wedding feast lasted three weeks.

When it was over, the king said, "You have done well, Mollie Whuppie, but you can do better. Did you see the giant's purse?"

"He hides it under his pillow."

"That purse is never empty. Steal it for me, and I'll marry your second sister to my second son."

"Done!" said Mollie Whuppie, and she changed her clothes and brushed her hair so that she looked unlike herself. Then, although her sisters wept, she ran lightly across Sword Bridge and into the forest.

When she knocked at the giant's door, the giant's wife still didn't know her.

"Come in," she said. "But be quiet. My man's in bed with a bad head."

All the while Mollie sat by the fire, the giant snored like a log being sawn. She sat until the giant's wife went out to shut up the hens, and then she crept over to the bed. Gently, gently, she slipped her hand under his pillow, until her fingers found the purse. Gently, gently, she pulled it out and made for the door.

But all the coins in the purse cried out, "Help! Help!" Up the giant woke, and up he sat, and he let a great roar out of him. But Mollie Whuppie was already running, and she ran and ran. The giant came after her in his nightshirt, trampling bushes and knocking down trees, but Mollie reached Sword Bridge first and ran lightly across, and the giant was afraid to follow.

"Death to you, Mollie Whuppie! Never come again!"

"Once more," she said, "once more."

She gave the purse to the king, and her second sister was married to the second prince, and the wedding feast lasted for two weeks.

When the feast was over, the king turned to Mollie once more, and said, "You have done well, Mollie Whuppie, but you can do better. Does the giant wear a ring?"

"It's never off his finger."

"That ring gives him long life. Steal it for me, and I'll marry you to my youngest son."

"Done!" said Mollie Whuppie, and she braided her hair and changed her clothes so that she looked unlike herself. Then, although both sisters wept and begged her not to go, she ran lightly across Sword Bridge and into the forest.

The giant's wife didn't know her and let her in when she knocked.

"But be quiet," she said. "My poor man's had so much trouble, he's gone to bed early."

So Mollie sat by the fire. But when the giant's wife stepped out for a moment, she upped from her stool and crept to the bed. Gently, gently, she reached under the covers and found the giant's hand. Gently, gently, she felt for the ring. Gently, gently, she slid it from his finger – but the giant woke up and gripped her little hand in his big one and yelled, "Got you!"

In came the wife, running.

"I know you, Mollie Whuppie!" said the giant. "Now, Mollie Whuppie, if I had done as much wrong to you as you've done to me, how would you pay me back?"

"I'd tie you in a sack, and then I'd cut a thick club and beat your bones with it," said Mollie Whuppie.

"And that's what I'll do to you!" said the giant, and he tied her in a sack and left her by the hearth while he went into the forest to cut a club.

The giant's wife sat by the fire, laughing, until

she heard Mollie Whuppie call, "Oh, if you could see what I can see! Oh, what I can see!"

"What can you see?"

"Oh, if only you could see!"

"Here, let me see!" And the giant's wife unfastened the sack, shook Mollie Whuppie out, and got in herself. Quick as a flash, Mollie tied up the sack and hid behind the door.

"I don't see anything," said the giant's wife.

Just then, in came the giant with half a tree as a club, and he thumped the sack, shouting, "That for my daughters! That for my bow! That for my purse!" He was shouting so much he never noticed it was his wife's voice crying out from the sack. Mollie Whuppie slipped from behind the door and ran. When the sack stopped moving, the giant opened it and found his wife, dead. Roaring with rage, he picked up his club and started after Mollie Whuppie.

But she was already across Sword Bridge and thumbing her nose at him. The giant was so angry that he ran across the bridge to get her. But he trod too heavily, and the sword-blade cut him into pieces, which fell into the chasm. And that was the end of the giant.

Mollie Whuppie climbed down into the chasm and took the ring off the giant's finger. She gave it to the king and was married to the youngest prince, and she never wanted for anything else.

Now pick the bones out of that!

135

HOW THE TORTOISE WAS DEFEATED BY HIS OWN MAGIC

Peggy Appiah

Although Kwaku Ananse, the spider, was very clever, he was also lazy, and, at times, when his plans went astray, he scarcely had enough for himself and his family to eat.

One year, Kwaku Ananse's crops failed, and since he had saved nothing, he was soon heavily in debt. He borrowed from the lion and from the leopard. He borrowed from the python and from the honey-badger, from the hare and from the lizard. Indeed, he borrowed from every animal in the kingdom, so that in the end he did not know where to look for money.

Each day, the animals came to his house to collect their debts, and at night they howled outside; so that he had to leave home and hide himself in the forest. After dark, he would creep back to his house for a meal and leave again in

the early morning, before the other animals reached his house.

Of course, since he was unable to stay at home or work on his farm, Kwaku Ananse could not make money to pay his debts, and he did not know which way to turn. One day, a stranger passing through the forest told him that the tortoise had the most wonderful magic, and if he could persuade him to give him some, all his troubles would be over.

Kwaku Ananse went off at once to look for the tortoise. He had nothing to take him but promises and a few dried palm kernels. He went deep into the forest, far away from the farms and villages, and at last came upon the tortoise in a cool and shady place, resting beneath the forest trees.

"Friend Tortoise," he said, "everyone says that you have the most wonderful magic and are the cleverest magician in the forest. Please help me. I am in debt to all the animals of the forest, and unless I can find some way to pay the debt, I don't know what I shall do. They won't even let me work on my farm."

"Dear, dear," said the tortoise. "I have indeed some magic which, though it does not make money, will make all the animals forget their debts. How much can you pay me for it?"

"Alas, Mr. Tortoise, I could bring you only these few palm kernels as a token. I have no money at all; but if you help me, I promise to work hard at my farm and I will come back in three months' time and give you all I have. I will swear an oath to do this."

The tortoise thought for a bit and then agreed. "You don't need to swear," he said, "I will take your word for it. Now, you swallow this liquid, and when the lion or the leopard or any other animal comes to ask you for money, you just say, 'Go hang!' to them, and start laughing, 'Ye, ye, ye, ye, ha, ha, ha, ho, ho, ho . . .' and they too will laugh and go away and forget all about the money."

Kwaku Ananse drank the medicine and went straight home. He told Aso, his wife, what had happened, and she sighed with relief. "At last, dear husband, we shall be free from worry, and you can earn something for us to live on."

Very soon, the animals, hearing that Kwaku was in his house, started to come and call on him.

At first, Kwaku Ananse scarcely dared to put his head outside the door, but Aso scolded him and, when the lion came, he plucked up courage and went to the door of the house. He opened the door just a little and asked the lion what he wanted.

"You know very well that you owe me, and that you must repay the debt. Otherwise, I shall be forced to eat you up."

Kwaku shook, but Aso prodded him in the back, and he said in a quavering voice, "Go . . . oo h . . . h. . . hang." The lion was furious and made ready to spring, but before he could do so, Kwaku Ananse opened his mouth and let out a rather shaky laugh.

"Ye, ye, ye, ye, he, he, he, he, ho, ho . . ." said Kwaku.

The lion started to grin, and then he burst out laughing, "Ye, ye, ye, ye, he, he, he, he, ho, ho. . ." He laughed till the forest around shook with laughter, and then he turned and loped off along the forest path, laughing as he went.

Kwaku Ananse gave a sigh of relief. The medicine had worked. He had been sweating profusely, for he had not quite believed that the magic could work. But after that, as each animal came to demand his money, Kwaku just said to him, "Go hang! . . .ye, ye, ye, ye, he, he, he, ho, ho . . ." and all the debts were forgotten. Some of the monkeys laughed so hard that you can still hear them to this day.

That night, Kwaku's throat was sore from laughing, but no one came to bother him any more.

He went back to work on the farm, and this time he was lucky and the season was a good one. He was able to sell his crops and even to save a little money.

After three months, Kwaku Ananse failed to visit the tortoise again. Now that he had saved a little, he did not want to give it all up. So he stayed at home and worked, and hoped that the tortoise would forget.

But the tortoise did not forget. After a bit, he came through the forest to see Kwaku Ananse.

"Friend Ananse," he said, "have the animals stopped troubling you? Did the medicine work? Why have you not been to pay me as you promised?"

Kwaku Ananse had no intention of paying. Remembering how successful the medicine had been with the other animals he thought, "Why not try it on the tortoise?"

"Go hang," he said, and opened his mouth to laugh again. "Ye, ye, ye, he, he, ha, ha, ho, ho . . ."

The tortoise looked puzzled, and then, despite himself, he started to laugh and laugh, "Ye, ye, ho, ho, ha, ha, he, he . . ." and off he waddled through the forest.

But the tortoise did not forget completely. The effects of the medicine wore off him in a few days, and he went back to Kwaku Ananse.

"Kwaku Ananse," he said accusingly, "you are wrong to treat me in this way, for was it not I who saved you from your debts? You are a most ungrateful creature. I suppose I have got what I deserve for trusting you. Give me my money, I pray."

But Kwaku just said, "Go hang . . .ye, ye, ye, ye, he, he, ho, ho . . ."

And the tortoise was forced to go off, laughing, through the forest. He had been made to feel the results of his own medicine.

RUMPELSTILTSKIN

Grimm Brothers

One day a king was riding through a village in his kingdom when he heard a woman singing,

"My daughter has burnt five cakes today,
My daughter has burnt five cakes today."

It was the miller's wife who was cross with her daughter for being so careless. The king stopped as he wanted to hear her song again. The miller's wife hoped to impress the king so she sang,

"My daughter has spun fine gold today,
My daughter has spun fine gold today."

And she boasted that her daughter could spin straw into gold thread.

The king was greatly impressed.

"If your daughter will spin for me in my palace, I'll give her many presents. I might even make her my queen," he announced.

"What a wonderful chance," muttered the miller's wife under her breath. "We'll all be rich." Then out loud she said, "My daughter will be honored, Your Majesty."

The king took the girl back to the palace and ordered a spinning wheel to be placed in a room filled with straw.

"Spin this into gold by the morning or I will chop off your head," he commanded.

Left alone, the poor girl wept bitterly. She could not spin straw into gold as her mother had boasted, nor could she escape, as the king had locked the door firmly behind him.

Suddenly, a little man appeared from nowhere. He had a small pointed face and wore elfin clothes in green and brown.

"What will you give me, pretty girl, if I spin this straw into gold for you?" he asked.

"I will give you my necklace," the girl replied. "But how can anyone spin straw into gold?"

The little man made no reply, but sat down at the spinning wheel and began to spin. By morning he had spun all the straw into fine gold thread. Then, with a skip and a hop and a stamp of his foot, he took the girl's necklace and disappeared.

When the king unlocked the room the next morning, he was astonished and delighted to see the skeins of golden thread. He had delicious food sent to the miller's daughter. But that evening he took her to another room with an even bigger pile of straw and a spinning wheel.

"Now, spin this into gold," he ordered, "and I shall reward you well. But if you fail, I shall chop off your head." And he walked out, locking the door firmly behind him.

The poor girl stared at the pile of straw and the spinning wheel. "What can I do?" she cried. "I cannot turn straw into gold, and the king will kill me if I fail."

Suddenly the same little old man in elfin clothes appeared before her.

"What will you give me this time if I spin your gold for you?" he asked.

"I'll give you my bracelet," said the miller's daughter, for she had nothing else to offer.

At once, the little old man sat down at the spinning wheel. All through the night he kept the spinning wheel whirring as he spun the straw into gold thread. He finished just before dawn and, snatching the bracelet, he disappeared, with a skip and a hop and a stamp of his foot.

The king was delighted the next morning, and sent pretty clothes and good food up to the girl as a reward.

"If this girl can really spin gold from straw," he thought greedily, "I shall always be rich if I make her my wife. But in case there is some trick, I will try her once more."

So that night, the king took the miller's daughter into a third room with an even bigger pile of straw and a spinning wheel.

"Spin this into gold," he commanded. "If you succeed, I shall marry you and you shall be my queen. If you fail, your head will be chopped off tomorrow."

Once more, as the girl wept bitterly before the pile of straw and the spinning wheel, the little man appeared from nowhere.

"I see you need my help again," he said. "How will you reward me this time if I save your life?"

"I have nothing more to give," the miller's daughter said sadly.

"Ah!" said the little man. "But if the straw is spun into gold tonight, you will become queen. Will you promise to give me your first child when it is born?"

"Yes! Yes!" cried the girl. She was sure that, when the time came, she would be able to save her child somehow.

So the little man sat and the spinning wheel whirred round and round. When dawn broke, all the straw had been turned into gold thread, and with a skip and a hop and a stamp of his foot, the little man disappeared once more.

The king was overjoyed when he saw the piles of glistening gold thread. He kept his promise and that very day the miller's daughter became his wife and queen.

The miller's daughter so enjoyed being queen, that she forgot all about her promise to the little man. About a year later, a fine son was born, and she was horrified when one day the little man appeared.

"I have come to claim the child you promised me," he said, stamping his foot as he spoke.

The queen pleaded with him to release her from the promise.

"Take my jewels and all this gold," she begged, "only leave me my little son."

The little man saw her tears and said, "Very well. You have three days in which to guess my name. You may have three guesses each night. If by the third night you have failed to guess my name, the baby is mine." Then he vanished.

The queen sent for her servants and ordered them to go throughout the kingdom asking if anyone had heard of the little man and if they knew his name.

That night, when the little man came, she tried some unusual names.

"Is it Caspar?" she asked.

"No!" he said, and stamped his foot in delight.

"Is it Balthazar?"

"No!" he cried, as he stamped his foot again.

"Is it Melchior?"

"No!" he cried. He stamped his foot and disappeared.

The next evening, the queen thought she would try some everyday names. So when the little man appeared, she asked, "Is your name John?"

"No!" he said, with his usual stamp.

"Is it Michael?"

"Is it James?"

"No! No!" he cried, stamping his foot each time. Then with a hop and a skip, triumphantly he disappeared.

The next day the palace servants returned without any news. The queen felt very sad, for she was sure that she would lose her baby son that night.

But just as the sun was setting and the little man was due to arrive, the last of the servants came rushing into the palace and hurried up to see the queen. He told her how he had traveled far and wide without success until, at the very edge of the kingdom, under the mountains, he had seen a little man singing as he danced around a fire.

"What did he sing?" asked the queen breathlessly.

> *"Today I brew, tomorrow I bake,*
> *Next day the queen's child I'll take.*
> *How glad I am that nobody knows*
> *My name is Rumpelstiltskin."*

The queen clapped her hands with joy and rewarded the servant. When the little man appeared, he asked if she had guessed his name.

"Is it Ichabad?" she asked.

"No!" he cried with pleasure, stamping his foot.

"Is it Carl?"

"No!" he shouted, as he laughed and stamped with glee.

"Is it . . ." the queen hesitated for a moment, ". . . is it Rumpelstiltskin?"

Now it was the queen's turn to laugh, for in a fit of rage, the little man stamped his foot so hard it went through the floor. He disappeared in a flash and was never seen again.

THE PUDDING LIKE A NIGHT ON THE SEA

Ann Cameron

"I'm going to make something special for your mother," my father said.

My mother was out shopping. My father was in the kitchen looking at the pots and the pans and the jars of this and that.

"What are you going to make?" I said.

"A pudding," he said.

My father is a big man with wild black hair. When he laughs, the sun laughs in the window-panes. When he thinks, you can almost see his thoughts sitting on all the tables and chairs. When he is angry, me and my little brother Huey shiver to the bottom of our shoes.

"What kind of pudding will you make?" Huey said.

"A wonderful pudding," my father said. "It will taste like a whole raft of lemons. It will taste like a night on the sea."

Then he took down a knife and sliced five lemons in half. He squeezed the first one. Juice squirted in my eye.

"Stand back!" he said, and squeezed again. The seeds flew out on the floor. "Pick up those seeds, Huey!" he said.

Huey took the broom and swept them up.

My father cracked some eggs and put the yolks in a pan and the whites in a bowl. He rolled up his sleeves and pushed back his hair and beat up the yolks. "Sugar, Julian!" he said, and I poured in the sugar.

He went on beating. Then he put in lemon juice and cream and set the pan on the stove. The pudding bubbled, and he stirred it fast. Cream splashed on the stove.

"Wipe that up, Huey!" he said.

Huey did.

It was hot by the stove. My father loosened his collar and pushed at his sleeves. The stuff in the pan was getting thicker and thicker. He held the beater up high in the air. "Just right!" he said, and sniffed in the smell of the pudding.

He whipped the egg whites and mixed them into the pudding. The pudding looked softer and lighter than air.

"Done!" he said. He washed all the pots, splashing water on the floor, and wiped the counter so fast his hair made circles around his head.

"Perfect!" he said. "Now I'm going to take a nap. If something important happens, bother me. If nothing important happens, don't bother me. And – the pudding is for your mother. Leave the pudding alone!"

He went to the living room and was asleep in a minute, sitting straight up in his chair.

Huey and I guarded the pudding.

"Oh, it's a wonderful pudding," Huey said.

"With waves on the top like the ocean," I said.

"I wonder how it tastes," Huey said.

"Leave the pudding alone," I said.

"If I just put my finger in – there – I'll know how it tastes," Huey said.

And he did it.

"You did it!" I said. "How does it taste?"

"It tastes like a whole raft of lemons," he said. "It tastes like a night on the sea."

"You've made a hole in the pudding!" I said. "But since you did it, I'll have a taste." And it tasted like a whole night of lemons. It tasted like floating at sea.

"It's such a big pudding," Huey said. "It can't hurt to have a little more."

"Since you took more, I'll have more," I said.

"That was a bigger lick than I took!" Huey said. "I'm going to have more again."

"Whoops!" I said.

"You put in your whole hand!" Huey said. "Look at the pudding you spilled on the floor!"

"I am going to clean it up," I said. And I took the sponge from the sink.

"That's not really clean," Huey said.

"It's the best I can do," I said.

"Look at the pudding!" Huey said.

It looked like the craters on the moon. "We have to smooth this over," I said, "so it looks the way it did before! Let's get spoons."

And we evened the top of the pudding with spoons, and while we evened it, we ate some more.

"There isn't much left," I said.

"We were supposed to leave the pudding alone," Huey said.

"We'd better get away from here," I said. We ran into our bedroom and crawled under the bed. After a long time, we heard my father's voice.

"Come into the kitchen, dear," he said. "I have something for you."

"Why, what is it?" my mother said, out in the kitchen.

Under the bed, Huey and I pressed ourselves to the wall.

"Look," said my father, out in the kitchen. "A wonderful pudding."

"Where is the pudding?" my mother said.

"WHERE ARE YOU BOYS?" my father said. His voice went through every crack and corner of the house.

We felt like two leaves in a storm.

"WHERE ARE YOU, I SAID!" My father's voice was booming.

Huey whispered to me, "I'm scared."

We heard my father walking slowly through the rooms.

"Huey!" he called. "Julian!"

We could see his feet. He was coming into our room.

He lifted the bedspread. There was his face, and his eyes like black lightning. He grabbed us by the legs and pulled. "STAND UP!" he said.

We stood.

"What do you have to tell me?" he said.

"We went outside," Huey said, "and when we came back, the pudding was gone!"

"Then why were you hiding under the bed?" my father said.

We didn't say anything. We looked at the floor.

"I can tell you one thing," he said. "There is going to be some beating here now! There is going to be some whipping."

The curtains at the window were shaking. Huey was holding my hand.

"Go into the kitchen!" my father said. "Right now!"

We went into the kitchen.

"Come here, Huey!" my father said.

Huey walked toward him, his hands behind his back.

"See these eggs?" my father said. He cracked them and put the yolks in a pan and set the pan on the counter. He stood a chair by the counter. "Stand up here," he said to Huey.

Huey stood on the chair by the counter.

"Now it's time for your beating!" my father said.

Huey started to cry. His tears fell in with the egg yolks.

"Take this!" my father said. My father handed him the eggbeater. "Now beat those eggs," he said. "I want this to be a good beating!"

"Oh!" Huey said. He stopped crying. And he beat the egg yolks.

"Now you, Julian, stand here!" my father said.

I stood on a chair by the table.

"I hope you're ready for your whipping!"
I didn't answer. I was afraid to say yes or no.
"Here!" he said, and he set the egg whites in
front of me. "I want these whipped and whipped
well!"

"Yes, sir!" I said, and started whipping.

My father watched us. My mother came into the kitchen and watched us.

After a while, Huey said, "This is hard work."

"That's too bad," my father said. "Your beating's not done!" And he added sugar and cream and lemon juice to Huey's pan and put the pan on the stove. And Huey went on beating.

"My arm hurts from whipping," I said.

"That's too bad," my father said. "Your whipping's not done."

So I whipped and whipped, and Huey beat and beat.

"Hold that beater in the air, Huey!" my father said.

Huey held it in the air.

"See!" my father said. "A good pudding stays on the beater. It's thick enough now. Your beating's done." Then he turned to me.

"Let's see those egg whites, Julian!" he said. They were puffed up and fluffy. "Congratulations, Julian!" he said. "Your whipping's done."

He mixed the egg whites into the pudding himself. Then he passed the pudding to my mother.

"A wonderful pudding," she said. "Would you like some, boys?"

"No, thank you," we said.

She picked up a spoon. "Why, this tastes like a whole raft of lemons," she said. "This tastes like a night on the sea."

Titles in the
Kingfisher Treasury series

ANIMAL STORIES

BALLET STORIES

BEDTIME STORIES

FIVE-MINUTE STORIES

FUNNY STORIES

GIANT AND MONSTER STORIES

PET STORIES

· PIRATE STORIES

PONY STORIES

PRINCESS STORIES

SPOOKY STORIES

STORIES FOR FOUR YEAR OLDS

STORIES FOR FIVE YEAR OLDS

STORIES FOR SIX YEAR OLDS

STORIES FOR SEVEN YEAR OLDS

STORIES FOR EIGHT YEAR OLDS